HARPER & MOON

RAMON ROYAL ROSS grew up on a fruit ranch in Walla Walla Valley. He lives with his youngest daughter, Lauren, and his mother, Wanda, in the foothills east of San Diego.

HARPER & MOON

RAMON ROYAL ROSS

AN AVON CAMELOT BOOK

HARPER & MOON is a work of fiction. Names, characters, places, and incidents
either are imagined or have been used fictitiously. Any resemblance to actual per-
sons, living or dead, is coincidental.

AVON BOOKS
A division of
The Hearst Corporation
1350 Avenue of the Americas
New York, New York 10019

Copyright © 1993 by Ramon Royal Ross
Published by arrangement with Bradbury Press
Library of Congress Catalog Card Number: 92-17216
ISBN: 0-380-72356-5
RL: 4.9

First Avon Camelot Printing: February 1995

CAMELOT TRADEMARK REG. U.S. PAT. OFF. AND IN OTHER COUNTRIES, MARCA REGISTRA-
DA, HECHO EN U.S.A.

Printed in the U.S.A.

OPM 10 9 8 7 6 5 4 3 2 1

For WJR—
the real Jewel

Contents

Map by Virginia Norey

1

The Sign Painter

Harper was only eight the last time he saw Paddie. It was an afternoon in early June, and the Walla Walla Valley was green and shimmering with summer heat. Harper was sitting on the front porch of the old farmhouse, doodling on the worn bricks with the damp end of a twig, bored, wishing for something exciting to happen, when he saw the sign painter's little delivery wagon turn in the lane and pull to a stop under the big maples. Harper hurried down the front walk to greet him.

Paddie flung himself out of the cab. "Sure and if it isn't young Harper himself," he said with a wink. "And gettin' better-lookin' all the time."

Harper couldn't remember the words ever changing, from visit to visit. He dug at the dirt with his toe.

The sign painter trotted to the back of the truck and opened the wide double doors. Shelves filled with paint cans and brushes and thinner and rags lined the dark interior walls. Cigarette smoke and the smell of whiskey and turpentine and perfume hung in the stale air.

At the far end of the wagon, dim in the light of a tiny kerosene lamp, was a narrow cot. That's where Paddie's wife, Tessie, sat, her ringed hands slowly shuffling and laying down cards covered with curious drawings. Blue smoke hid her face. Over the years, Harper never once saw her leave her bed. Never, that is, until later, that same June day.

"I knew ye'd be watchin' for us," Paddie said. "And I says to Tessie, I says, 'We must be bringin' the lad a bit of a treat'—Didn't I say that now, love?" Paddie turned toward the still figure inside the wagon.

Harper sneaked a glance at Tessie. She never even looked up.

Paddie slapped at his shirt and trouser pockets. "Now, where'd I go and put it?" he muttered, scratching his head. He leaped up into the truck, shifting bottles and cans about.

"It's gone!" he yelped finally. "Some blaggard's robbed me of yer treat, when me back was turned. And that after I'd hauled it all the way from Pendleton."

Hands trembling, he patted Harper's shoulders. Harper squirmed with delight, smelling the smoke and whiskey. Oh, wasn't Paddie a prince of a man!

"What?" Paddie asked. "What's this?" He pulled a little white crumpled sack from the bib of Harper's overalls. "Why, ye young rascal! So ye're the one! It's tricked me ye have, climbin' up in the wagon and takin' yer present when I wasn't lookin'! Now what kind of a wicked lad must ye be, to play a prank like that?"

How the sack got in his overalls, Harper could never figure out. But that didn't matter. He'd managed, somehow, to fool Paddie again.

"Open it! Open it!" Paddie shouted in delight.

Always the bag held the same thing: a handful of candy corn kernels, smelling of turpentine. Afterward, whenever Harper smelled turpentine, he'd remember Paddie, and Tessie, and the awful way that day had ended.

"Now, lad, ye can plant these few candy kernels, and next year have yerself an entire field, filled with the finest corn imaginable. Or ye can be a greedy child, and eat them now, savin' none for tomorrow. Which'll it be?"

"Eat them now!"

"Eh? How's that?" Paddie paused. Then, "Good lad! The very decision I'd have made meself. For who knows what tomorrow will bring? And now I'd best be gettin' to work, or yer father'll send me packin'!"

Hopping in and out of the truck, dropping brushes and paints, cursing himself happily for his clumsiness, Paddie set up his easel and paints. When everything was ready, he poked his head inside once more. "Tessie, darlin'," he said, "I'm startin' work. Can I be gettin' ye anything first?"

Harper stole another glance at Tessie. Maybe this time she'd answer. But no, only the same slow, dreamy, sliding movement of card laid on card; it was as if Paddie hadn't spoken.

"Have a good rest then."

Paddie rolled a cigarette and seated himself on his stool. He dipped his shaking brush in a jar of paint.

Munching candy corn, Harper watched, fascinated, as the brush wobbled its way toward the sign board. At the very last minute, when it seemed as if paint would fly everywhere, a line of bright color appeared.

Paddie painted another line, and another. Beautifully colored fruits and strange, wonderful letters and words began to stir and shift, almost as if they'd been there all the time, waiting for the brush to give them life.

"Aye, lad," Paddie said with a sigh, half to Harper and half to himself. " 'Tis a grand invention, paint, and a board to smear it on. Would that the rest of the world could be so easily arranged."

2

Blood Brothers

Paddie and Tessie had a son named Moon. When Harper was eight, Moon was thirteen—maybe fourteen—no one seemed quite sure. Harper never saw Moon riding in his father's truck. But half an hour or so after the sign painter had started work, he'd catch sight of Moon climbing over Eiffort's pasture fence. He'd see the shock of hair, coarse as a horse's mane, the dark, thin face, the ragged overalls and faded shirt, the narrow feet, bare and hard as horn. Harper would run to meet him.

Always Moon carried treasures he'd picked up along the way: a tiny dead featherless newborn bird with dull purple skin and a beak yellow as brass; the filmy sheddings of a garter snake; a robin's pale blue egg with a tiny hole at one end.

Moon's voice exploded when he talked: high, scrunched-up little bursts of garbled speech. "Snake do that," he'd said the day he brought the egg. "Climb tree. Suck out baby bird so quiet that old mother bird never know he there. Then snake go. Mother look at egg. Baby gone. Mother bird cry. But then forget. No cry no more."

Sometimes Moon gave Harper toys he'd made: cars with bottle tops for wheels; dull black wooden pistols that shot rubber bands; Quaker Oats containers that rolled away, paused, and then mysteriously returned.

If they were close enough for Paddie to hear them talking, the painter would glance up from his work.

"Be off with ye," he'd say to Moon, his voice harsh. "And stop yer crazy prattlin'. Yer mother's trying to rest. Ye hear me now?"

Then he'd look at Harper and the smile would come back to his face. "Aye, lad, don't ye be listenin' to the poor dumb fool. Can't talk straight, he can't. And don't know what he's sayin', either, half the time. He ain't quick, like ye."

Moon's face would darken. But then he'd grin that funny, crooked grin of his.

"Come on, Harp!" he'd say. "Go play in creek!"

That June day, half an hour after Paddie had begun work, Moon came loping across the pasture, carrying a sailboat he'd made. Harper ran to see it.

"Come on, Harp," Moon said, taking care to stay out of Paddie's sight. "We take her down to creek. Sail her."

Moments later the two of them were standing ankle deep in mud among the buttercups and forget-me-nots, the cool mud oozing between their bare toes, the smell of peppermint in their noses, listening to the drowsy gurgle of water drifting past. The creek made a lazy turn there, forming a little pool half-shaded by alders, before flowing on under the footbridge.

The hull of the boat was a one-by-six pine board, perhaps two feet long, pointed at one end. The masts were cedar, probably split from a fence post. The cabin was a block of pine with circles of black paint for portholes, the keel a piece of tin cut from a can. Another scrap of tin, fastened to the stern, served as a clumsy rudder.

But the sails were beautiful. They were some fine, thin fabric, pale and smooth as rose petals. Just looking at them made Harper want to touch them.

Cradling the little craft in his arms, Moon waded in, not even bothering to roll up his pants legs. He didn't stop until he reached the middle of the pond, the water up to his waist. He shivered. "Cold."

After he'd adjusted the rudder and sails, he wetted a finger and held it up. "Wind," he said, nodding toward the west. Harper couldn't feel a breath of air.

Holding the boat, Moon waded toward the footbridge. When he reached it, he turned and faced upstream. The creek was wide and sluggish here, with almost no current. The far bank, indented with little coves and overhung with tufts of grass, was a good fifty feet away.

Harper felt a brief stirring in the air and a coolness on his cheek. A light breeze scurried by, scuffing the smooth surface of the creek. Moon held on to the boat a second longer, then let go.

For what seemed like an eternity the little craft sat there, not moving. But then, with a silky rustle, the sails began to fill. They fell slack, then filled again. And then, slowly, with great majesty, the little ship began to move; sailing, sailing, upstream!

Watching it, Harper could feel the world he knew—the creek and the pasture and the orchard—disappearing. He was far away, on some strange sea. Heavy sails slapped overhead, and seabirds cried. His face was wet with salt spray, and he could look down, and see, far below, in the dark waters, fishes, flashing like moonbeams.

"Harp! Hey!"

Dazed, Harper saw the stream and the footbridge and the packing shed. And Moon, waist deep in the middle of the stream, shouting at him and pointing.

"Other side! Bring her back when she make shore."

Pulling free of the black mud, Harper ran across the bridge, ducking under the branches of the alder tree, reaching the far side of the creek just in time to see the boat nudging like a pup at the bank below. Flopping down on his belly, he lifted it from the water.

"Goes good, hey?" Moon shouted.

Harper tried to answer but no words came. He carried the boat across the bridge as if it were some fine treasure and set it down among the cress and sedge and forget-me-nots at the water's edge. "What's her name?" he asked finally.

Moon shrugged. "What you want to call her?"

"Well," Harper said, hesitating, "you could call her *Tessie,* after your mother."

Moon's face grew dark. "You think I name my ship after that old boozer?"

Harper remembered the dim interior of the wagon, the

flickering lamp, the smoke, Tessie's restless hands moving the cards.

"I don't know. . . . *Speedy* . . . *Racer* . . . ?"

Moon thought for a moment. He shook his head. No.

A hummingbird darted past the two of them, lighting for a second on the head of a thistle, its wings a blur, before hurrying off. They watched as it climbed higher and higher into the sky.

Moon pulled a crumpled rose, dried and nearly black, from his overalls pocket. Holding the flower in his hand, he held out his arm and made a high-pitched, hollow, half-whistling sound.

The bird was hovering over their heads, at least thirty feet away, its throat a smudge of red, shimmering with ruby light. It darted closer, and then, trusting as a tame canary, lit on Moon's open palm and poked its beak in among the rose petals. After a few seconds, it raised its head, tilting it back so that its red throat shone like a jewel. Harper could feel the fierce look in its eye. Oh, it was handsome!

Now the bird was gone, flying toward the ship. It touched the sails, then landed, like a figurehead, on the prow.

How long it remained there was always a mystery to Harper. A minute? A day? It didn't matter. Years later, he could still hold that memory up and see the scene as clearly as one sees fruit preserved in a jar.

But the bird was gone, and he hadn't seen it go. He heard Moon's voice, soft. *"Ruby."* He grabbed Harper by the arm. "But that secret name."

Harper nodded.

"*Hummingbird*. That name we tell. Okay?" He gripped Harper's arm tighter.

Harper nodded again. He gulped. His heart was thumping like an engine.

"Give me your hand."

Moon pulled a needle from the bib of his overalls, jabbing with it at the end of Harper's thumb. He did the same with his own thumb, then slid the needle back into his overalls.

"Don't hurt," he said. He pressed Harper's thumb with a finger until a drop of blood appeared, then did the same with his own thumb.

"Now," he said, "hold together."

Harper felt dizzy. The pressure on his finger was almost more than he could bear. Some animal, hot and heavy with blood, was pressing against him.

Then it was over.

He looked around. The dizziness was gone. The sky was still and blue. A few soft clouds were making their way east, toward the Blue Mountains. The alder trees stirred. He could hear the slow murmur of the creek. Behind him, up the meadow past the crab apple tree, sat the big gray-shingled house, safe and snug under the silver maples.

And there was Moon, thin and brown and tall, sucking his finger to clean the blood from it. Harper popped his own finger in his mouth, tasting the salty taste of blood and creek mud.

"Brothers now," Moon said. "Have same blood. Now you never tell secret name."

He grinned his crooked grin. Then he spoke again, all the darkness gone from his voice. "Come on! We sail *Hummingbird*. Sail her clear to China. Okay?"

It was late afternoon, the best time of the day, when the two of them headed back up the path to the house, Harper trotting to keep up with Moon's long stride. In the distance, a cow mooed, the sound sweet and peaceful. The wind stirred the maples, and the leaves trembled, showing their pale, silvery backsides.

Paddie was standing by his truck, washing out his brushes. When he saw them, he leaned inside. They could hear him saying something.

"Talking to that old witch," Moon muttered to Harper, plopping down on the limp grass in front of the house. "She prob'ly so drunk she can't hear."

Paddie was fussing with the brushes again. He put them away, then filled a tin basin with water and washed his hands. When he was done, he rolled a cigarette and lit it, inhaling a deep breath of smoke. Harper had seen him work his way through this same ritual before, but it always fascinated him; the deliberate care Paddie gave to things.

"Yer mother's been asking for ye," the sign painter called to Moon. He turned back to the truck. "Tessie, he's here."

The truck swayed. A small, heavy glass rolled out the door and tumbled to the ground.

"Moon? You—stay!" A voice, thin and high, but filled with such force that Harper couldn't move, came from inside. He heard the shuffle of slippers. Tessie, leaning heavily on a cane, her breath whistling in her throat, appeared at the back of the truck. A short quilted housecoat was wrapped around her thick body. Her legs were frail, clad in dark cotton stockings. But it was her eyes that held Harper's gaze; they were almost black, with no light coming from them.

Paddie had begun polishing a truck fender. He looked over at Harper and smiled, that easy, sly smile of his. "Now, Harper, lad," he said in his rich, pleasing voice, "did ye get a demonstration in the manly art of sailing?"

"Shut up!" Tessie hissed. "Shut up, and help me down. And you! Moon! Come here!"

3

Tessie

Clutching her cane, Tessie shuffled unsteadily to the open door. She stood for a moment, weaving back and forth, then started to climb down. Her slipper caught against the sill. With a heavy grunt, she tumbled and fell to the ground, her thin legs flailing the air, sending the second slipper flying.

Paddie rushed to her side. "Tessie! Love! Are ye hurt?"

Tessie struck at him with her cane. "Help me up, you fool! No! Not that way! You'll pull my arm off!"

Sweat broke out on Paddie's face.

"There, there," he muttered, trying awkwardly to lift her.

At last Tessie was on her feet again. Impatiently, she shoved Paddie away with the pink rubber tip of her cane. She yanked her beads back in place around her neck and straightened her long gray braided hair. Her eyes darted about. "My slipper," she wheezed. "Where's my slipper? Bring me my slipper."

Paddie hurried to fetch it.

"Not you! Moon! You! Bring me my slipper."

Harper watched, scarcely daring to breathe. For a long time Moon didn't move. Then, slowly, he walked toward the slipper, shoved at it with his toe, and kicked it in her direction.

"No!" she said. "Pick it up!"

Another long pause. Finally, Moon bent down and picked up the slipper.

"Bring it here!"

Moon walked toward her. Harper had never seen anyone move slower.

"Put it on."

Moon knelt and worried the slipper back on her foot.

"Thank you," she said, her voice heavy with sarcasm. "And now, I'd like to see that boat of yours."

Moon shook his head.

"You heard me. Bring it here!"

Moon came back to where Harper sat. He picked up the boat and walked back toward her, stopping several feet away.

"Closer! What's the matter with you? Think I'll bite?"

Moon took another step. Harper watched, unable to move. Something terrible was about to happen.

"You afraid of your own mother? Come here, I said! There! That's better!" Leaning against her cane, Tessie reached out and touched the boat with gnarled fingers. Her silver rings glinted in the light. "So," she said, her voice rich and sweet, "been making more toys—now, isn't that nice."

Paddie had returned to his aimless polishing. "Father," she said to him, "isn't it a wonder what this boy of ours can do?" Paddie nodded. Heavy stains showed under his arms.

"—Take that board. I'd not be surprised but that you found it lying alongside the road, or in some old pile of lumber."

No answer.

"And the masts. Split from a fence post—and no harm to anyone."

Harper couldn't take his eyes off her. She seemed like some huge, puffy snake, preparing to strike.

"String—and old tin cans—I tell you, Father, the boy's a regular genius for finding things."

She paused, then began to finger the sails, like a woman in a store, considering a garment. "Tell me now," she said, "where ever did you find these sails? Why, they're silk, I'd say, from the feel of them. And I know cloth."

Moon's trouser legs had begun to tremble.

Tessie turned to Paddie again. "Well, Father," she said in that same rich, heavy tone, "we have a little mystery here. Such beautiful sails, and our boy so proud of them— and yet, he can't tell us where they came from."

Suddenly, the cane whistled through the air, striking Moon on the arm. "They're mine!" Tessie howled. "You stole them! You stole them from me when I was sleeping. Stole them! Handkerchiefs woven from the purest silk and given to me by my mother, and you stole them! Isn't that so?"

The cane slashed again, cutting across Moon's shoulder.

His head jerked. He stumbled and fell moaning to the ground, curling himself around the boat to protect it. Tessie kicked him and lifted the cane to strike again. "Get up, you thief!" she shrieked. Spittle flew from her mouth. "Get up, so I can see your ugly face!"

Harper ran up the front walk and into the house. Jewel, his mother, was in the kitchen, peeling potatoes. With a cry he threw himself at her, hugging her cotton dress.

"Moon! It's Moon! She's killing him!"

Jewel pushed him aside and ran out of the house and down the front walk. "Stop that!" she said, her voice ringing like a trumpet.

The ribbon had slipped from Tessie's braid, and a dirty pink satin slip showed where her housecoat had fallen open. Her body rose and fell with the effort of her breathing. "You keep out of this, you bloody witch!" she said, striking Jewel across the cheek. A red welt appeared.

Jewel grabbed the cane. Tessie tumbled to the ground like a june bug, her legs sprawling up in the air, the curdy white flesh of her thighs showing above the black rolled line of her stockings. Jewel stood over her, the cane raised high above her head. Her dark hair had come loose and circled her face. Her breath came in spasms.

"No!" Paddie shouted. "For the love of God! No!"

For a dazed second Jewel stood there. Then, with a cry, she threw the cane into the wagon.

"Get her out of here," she said. "Get her out! Before I do something terrible to her."

Paddie was bending over Tessie. "Oh, my darlin', my poor darlin'. . . ," he crooned. Tessie kicked at him with her withered legs. "He stole them," she howled. "The most beautiful thing I owned, and he stole them. . . ."

Paddie climbed inside the wagon and returned with a quilt. He flung it over her. "There, there," he said. "It's rest you're needin'—I'll have ye back in yer own bed in a jiffy, where ye belong. And a wee somethin' to warm ye."

Jewel was kneeling beside Moon, smoothing his coarse dark hair with her hand. Blood seeped through the arm of his shirt, and a thick red welt ran along his cheek. His eyes were squeezed shut.

"Lie still," she said. "I'll get some warm water and some bandages."

Moon shook his head. Slowly, he raised himself to his hands and knees. Blood oozed from the cut on his cheek. Blood dripped from his ear and nose. His shirt was ripped across the back. One strap from his overalls had been torn loose. Grabbing a truck fender for support, he struggled to his feet. He shook his head and tried to grin.

"Whooeee!" he said weakly. "Old witch sure can hit!"

He stood for a moment, then took a step, his bare feet slapping at the dusty grass. He stopped and looked at Jewel and Harper, blood dripping from his lip.

"Don't feel too pert."

He took another step, and another. When he reached the little rise by the pump house, he turned and made a jerky bow.

"Thank you, ma'am, for takin' her off 'a me. I don't forget that."

Jewel nodded. Harper felt her arm around his shoulder,

and the warmth of her thigh as she pressed him to her.

Moon was staggering across the field toward Eiffort's fence. He stopped again and turned toward them. "Hey! Harp!" he called. "You keep *Hummingbird*. Okay?" He limped on, crawled under the fence, then slowly rose to his feet and disappeared behind Eiffort's barn, heading toward the cottonwoods that marked the Walla Walla River.

Minutes later, the little green truck rolled out the lane, raising a veil of dust that drifted across the salt grass pasture. Harper felt Jewel's hand tighten on his shoulder. There was a long silence. "Well, I guess I'd better get supper started," she said finally. "The men'll be coming in from the orchard before long." She hugged Harper, a hard, fierce hug. "That poor, poor boy," he heard her murmur, more to herself than to him.

For a long time, Harper sat by himself on the front porch, staring off toward the thin purple line of the Blue Mountains, kicking at a crack in the bricks where the mortar was working loose.

Why hadn't he been the one to stop Tessie! Instead of running to his momma, like a crybaby!

Some of the mortar was free now. He picked up a piece and threw it across the shaggy lawn toward the freshly painted signs. Then, getting to his feet, he walked over to where they stood, leaning like grave markers against the base of the big maple tree. CANTELOUPES, PEACHES, RASP-BERRIES—the print read. The painted fruits gleamed, juicy and ripe, on the white boards; and the words, green and gold, slithered like grass snakes across the smooth wood.

That Paddie, with his slippery talk and his clever brush! Not lifting a hand to help his own son! He hated him! Hated him even more than he hated Tessie. And he hated her more than anyone! More than Hitler, even!

Scooping up a handful of dirt, he threw it at the signs. Then, cradling the boat in his arms, he crept up to his room, where he laid it on top of his bookcase. *Ruby* was safe. That much, at least, he could do for Moon. That, and wait. Someday, maybe, he'd do more.

A week later, in the middle of the night, Paddie's truck veered off a gravel road in the wheat hills of Walla Walla, near Starbuck, plunged a hundred and fifty feet down a cliff, and ended up in the Palouse River. A rancher, out early the next morning, looking for a strayed milk cow, peered over the edge and spotted the truck, upside down in six feet of muddy yellow spring runoff.

Paddie and Tessie were still inside; Paddie in the cab, Tessie in back. Both of them were dead. Drowned, the coroner's report read. "Prob'ly drunk," Shorty, the hired man, added. "Bet a dollar they never knew what happened, either one of 'em!"

Suddenly, without wanting to, Harper remembered Paddie's little kindnesses—the candy corn, the sly talk, the clever tricks. He wanted Paddie back—that Paddie, the funny one—alive and gnomish, who could coax pictures out of thin air. Not the other one. Not the cruel one. Not the coward who wouldn't even stand up for his own son. That one he hated. That one he would always hate.

Moon didn't show up at the farm for more than a month.

Then, one afternoon, there he came, loping across the pasture. His cheek was nearly healed. He dug in his pocket for a strange purple stone he'd brought along for Harper. Shy as a suitor, he handed Jewel a bouquet of wildflowers. She asked him if he needed a place to stay.

He shook his head.

She insisted on making him a sandwich. He ate it in two great bites, then wiped his mouth with his sleeve. He nodded his thanks.

From time to time after that he'd drop in for a few minutes, always with a gift of some sort: wild roses for Jewel, a yellow glass reflector for Harper, a cupful of black-berries, a single perfect tail feather from a Chinese pheas-ant, a worn paper sack filled with tiny wild winter banana apples. Sometimes he'd spend the afternoon making a toy for Harper: a slingshot, a shingle dart, a paddle boat that flip-flopped its way across the bathtub. He'd eat supper with the family at the kitchen table, the lamps gleaming, the rich steamy smells of food filling the air.

"Stay the night," Harper's father, Walter, would urge. "There's plenty of room out in the bunkhouse, if you can put up with Shorty's snoring."

Shorty would nod in agreement. "And don't listen to Walter, there. He don't know what he's saying. Why, I'm quiet as a baby."

Moon would grin and shake his head. Thanks, but no, he'd be going.

Three years passed; four. Now and then, during haying, or just before the picking season, Walter would hire Moon for a few days. He'd work, but almost as a favor. Money just didn't seem to matter to him. Finally, Walter stopped asking.

Where he lived or how, no one knew. Oh, there were lots of places he could have hidden out: abandoned farmhouses, old cellars. Maybe he'd made a den in one of those. Harper wanted to ask him. But always something held him back.

And the little ship? It sat, all those years, on top of Harper's bookshelf. Once, remembering the way it had sailed that day in June, he carried it down to the creek. A light breeze was blowing down from the Horse Heaven Hills; perfect weather. But the silken sails drooped and the boat refused to budge. He gave it a nudge, and it tipped over. He picked it out of the water; the sails wet rags; the hull a crude pine board.

Maybe he'd imagined that whole afternoon, so long ago.

4

Olinger

Late in the summer Harper turned twelve—the summer after Pearl Harbor—Olinger sent word down the mountain asking if Harper wanted to spend a week or so up at the store.

For as long as Harper could remember, when Walter and Shorty were heading up to the Blue Mountains to cut a load of wood on the old Home Place, they'd let him ride along. On the way back down they'd always stop in at Olinger's Store for sardines and crackers, soda pop for Harper and a bottle of beer for the men.

Olinger, who'd lived alone up in the Blues now for more than twenty years—ever since he'd come back from the army, during the First World War—had a soft spot for Harper. He'd dig out a licorice strap from the fly-specked glass jar on the store counter in the back of his cabin.

"Now eat that, and try not to think what color it's turning your insides," he'd say, trying to act gruff.

Harper would sit on the worn plank floor listening to

the comforting sound of man talk, secretly investigating the dark, mysterious interior of the cabin, with its snowshoes and skis in one corner, Olinger's carvings of birds and animals on the high shelves, the big sled lying atop the rafters, the wall pegs heaped with the old man's winter mackinaw and checkered shirts, the store counter—its shelves scattered with a few canned goods. Olinger's cot sat in one corner, with a stack of books and magazines piled alongside. Even if the day was warm, there'd be a fire in the big black kitchen stove. Toward evening, a kerosene lantern would cast eerie shadows. Always the cabin smelled of coffee and wood smoke and bacon and tobacco and kerosene. Beneath all those smells were other faint, ancient smells; the smells of logs and moss and mice.

"Can I go?"

Walter nodded. "I don't know why not. The work's pretty well caught up around here. And I can't think of anyone I'd rather have you spend time with. Better take the tent. That cabin's pretty small. You get yourself packed this afternoon, and your mother and I'll run you up there tomorrow morning. That all right with you, Jewel?"

By noon the next day they were pulling the Oldsmobile to a stop in the meadow fronting Olinger's. The dark firs stood tall and melancholy above the low cabin, and the little meadow was bright with camas and skunk cabbage and Indian paintbrush. Olinger was sitting in an old chair by the cabin door, whittling. He looked up. "Look who's here!" he shouted.

Even at that distance Harper could see—or thought he could see—Olinger's eyes crinkling up in a smile. Olinger was dressed the same as always: black canvas logger pants, cut short over his laced moccasin boots, a faded blue work shirt, and a sweat-stained fedora with a blue jay feather stuck in the hatband. His face was brown and weathered, his mustache as big and carefully tended as ever. Limping a bit, he strode across the meadow to greet them; a small man, lean, surprisingly boyish.

"He's aged, hasn't he?" Jewel said to Walter. She rolled down her window.

"Nonsense! Besides, he's no spring chicken. You just don't see him that often, like I do. He looks just fine."

"Hush! He'll hear you."

Olinger had reached the car. He peered inside, doffed his hat and bowed to Jewel and kissed her hand, then stood, smiling, shaking his head in mock sorrow.

"What a pity," he said. "Wasting your glories on that bald-headed farmer."

"Oh, you!" Jewel laughed. "Still the old flatterer!"

Pulling his big gold railroad watch out of his shirt pocket, Olinger flipped open the lid, glanced down, snapped the lid shut, and put the watch back. He leaned across Jewel and shook hands with Walter. "Eleven fifty-eight. You made good time. Must have knowed you were having venison steaks for lunch. And morels. Picked them this morning. Now get out of the car, all of you!" He pounded Harper on the back. "Why don't you run fetch that root beer I put in the spring."

The clear air smelled of ripe berries and hot gravel and pine resin. The sky was the darkest blue Harper could remember. A woodpecker drummed on a distant tree.

Soon the smell of wood smoke and venison steaks floated through the air. Jewel had brought an apple pie. "Nice and tart," she said to Olinger, "the way you like it."

"Didn't think you'd remember."

A car rumbled past on the dirt road, raising a thin cloud of dust. The driver waved. "Don't get much business," Olinger said with a shrug, watching it disappear. "But that suits me. Can't imagine running a store where you had to stop what you were doing all the time to wait on folks."

And then it was time to say good-bye. Jewel kissed Harper. "Don't forget to change your underwear! And your socks! And mind Olinger." Walter hugged him, awkwardly. "Take care of yourself, son," he said.

Olinger handed a paper bag to Jewel. "Mushrooms," he said. "For you two and Shorty." Car doors slammed. The Oldsmobile turned around in the meadow, flowers and grass bending under the tires. Harper watched the car disappear, leaving a trail of dust. He waved. He stood for a few seconds more, then turned back toward the cabin.

Olinger was standing in the doorway.

"Feeling a little blue, all of a sudden, I betcha," he said.

Harper had a lump in his throat. He nodded his head.

"I felt the same way, the first time I was away from home." Olinger began clearing dishes from the rough table. "Tell you what," he said, "you pitch your tent while I clean up this mess. Then we'll take a hike out to Target Meadows, see if we can find a few huckleberries for supper. Last week, when I was there, they was just starting in."

Harper set to work. He heard Olinger fetch water from the spring. A blue jay began to scold. He'd just pounded in the last tent stake and crawled inside, smelling the warm oiled canvas, feeling homesick, to lay out his bedroll, when he heard a footstep outside. He figured it was Olinger. The tent flap opened.

"Hey! Harp!"

Moon, a bedroll slung over his shoulder, stood hunched in the opening, grinning at him.

Harper yipped for joy. "How'd you get here?"

"Hiked. Olinger say you'd be here. So I come too."

"But it's twenty-five miles! And we didn't pass you on the road."

Moon shrugged. "Shortcuts."

Thus began ten happy days. In the evenings, after supper, they'd sit outside, watching the stars, listening to the hoot of owls and the far-off songs of coyotes. Sometimes Olinger would tell stories: of peculiar happenings up in the Blues; or about Montana, where one winter he and Shorty tended a herd of wild cayuses, the thermometer steady at forty below. Once Harper asked Olinger to tell about when he'd been in France, during the First World War. There was a silence. Olinger cleared his throat. "Why don't I tell you about the time your daddy and me worked in the sawmills over on the coast, instead. I do believe you'd find that more interesting."

In the mornings Harper would wake to the sound of Olinger clattering the stove lids. Moon would most likely be already off on some mysterious errand of his own. A few minutes later there'd be the smell of wood smoke and coffee brewing. The three of them would down a cup of coffee, thick with evaporated milk and sugar, then hike out to the Far Point, Olinger limping, wheezing a bit whenever the trail climbed a little.

"Danged knee," he'd mutter at exactly the same place in the trail, every time they passed.

Moon and Harper would grin at each other. They knew he'd say that.

When they reached the Point, Olinger would lean back against a shale outcropping, pull his pipe out of his mackinaw pocket, and light it. He'd gaze due west, past the thickets of chokecherry, past the wheat stubble and scattered pines, past the Walla Walla Valley, to the Horse Heaven Hills beyond.

"Been making this same hike, winter and summer, ever since I got back from the war, twenty-five years ago," he'd say. "And I don't believe I've ever seen those hills look the same way twice; purple . . . green . . . gold . . . brown . . . white . . . they remind me sometimes of a pretty woman, dressin' up different every day, just to please herself."

He'd dig in his shirt pocket for his watch. Harper remembered, when he was little, Olinger letting him hold that watch; heavy, warm, smooth, golden—the most beautiful object he'd ever seen. On the back was Olinger's name in engraved script: John Quincy Olinger. Harper had learned to tell time when he was five, leaning against Olinger's bony shoulder, listening to Olinger's patient instruction.

"We made good time. I'll bet you boys think you're

smart, pushing an old man like that! Well, we'll see! I'll make you sweat on the way back, by golly.''

One morning Olinger pointed west with the stem of his pipe to a thin silver thread on the horizon. "See that? That's the Columbia River. Must be eighty miles away.'' He paused. "One morning some years ago—winter, so cold I could scarcely catch my breath—I seen Mount Hood, and Mount Adams, and Mount Rainier, clean across the state, floating in the sky, so close I could have reached out and touched them! I've never forgotten the sight!''

Once, watching him, Harper saw a sadness—gone as quickly as it had come—pass across Olinger's face. "Another war,'' Olinger muttered, half to himself. "And a scant twenty years since the last one.'' He shook his head. "Don't seem like we ever learn.''

Moon's hand reached out and rested on the old man's shoulder. Harper noticed, for the first time, how tall Moon had grown. But then, after all, he must be close to eighteen; a man, practically.

Some mornings, they'd hike out to Target Meadows to pick huckleberries, pungent and dark. Olinger showed them how to mix the berries with dried venison and bacon grease to make pemmican. "It's not bad,'' he said. "But you can get awful tired of it. Back in Montana, that winter I told you about, when Shorty and me were batching together, I do believe we'd have traded everything we had for a meal of something besides pemmican.''

One day Moon and Harper dammed up the spring and

dug out a place deep enough to swim a few strokes. The water was icy cold. They begged Olinger to come in with them, but he said he'd be blamed if he would; he was too old for that sort of foolishness. Later, while he was taking a nap, the two of them sneaked up on him. They carried him, protesting, to the pond, and threw him in, clothes and all. Olinger staggered out, sputtering, wheezing. "You're in for it now," he said, "you young hooligans! I've served you fair warning!"

One afternoon, late, far from the cabin, at the rim of a canyon, they saw a bull elk silhouetted against the evening sky, a quarter of a mile away. A luminous haze surrounded the animal. It lifted its head. Long seconds later they heard its call trumpeting across the hills. Harper blinked. When he looked again, the elk had disappeared, even while its cry still echoed.

The morning after seeing the elk, Harper woke to the sound of Olinger inside the cabin, rattling the stove lids, as usual. He heard the squeak of the door, and the splash of a bucket. Drowsily, he glanced over to see if Moon was still sleeping. But he was gone; his bedroll gone. Harper pulled on his trousers, and headed for the cabin.

Olinger looked up. "Gone?"

Harper nodded.

Olinger measured coffee grounds into the pot and set it on the stove. He added a couple of sticks of wood to the firebox. He dipped a big spoon into the coffee pot, stirring the grounds around. "I had the feeling, last night, he'd be headin' out."

"You mean he didn't tell you good-bye?"

Olinger shook his head. "Nope." He stirred the coffee again. "That's not Moon's way."

The long day passed. That evening the two of them sat at the supper table, spooning up the last can of peaches. The night air was chill, and the heat from the stove felt good. A moth circled the lamp chimney. Harper asked a question he'd had on his mind for a long time.

"How long have you known Moon?"

Olinger leaned back in his chair, scraping the bowl of his pipe, making a neat pile of charred bits next to his plate. It took several minutes before he answered.

"Must have been, maybe, thirteen years ago," he said finally. "Before you were born. Paddie and Tessie had just moved into the valley, and Paddie was on his way back to Walla Walla from La Grande. He'd had a job there. Stopped by, pretty well lit, staggering across the meadow, singing 'Mother McCree.' "

Olinger smiled, remembering.

"Moon couldn't have been more'n four or five at the time. What a sight! Barefooted. Hair like a cayuse's mane. Long legged as a colt. Coming across the meadow behind Paddie—him not even knowing the boy was there. And Moon finding things to look at every step . . . a feather . . . a handful of grass . . . flowers. He'd made himself a headband by the time he was halfway to the store.

"Paddie slapped some money down. Said he'd run out of tobacco. Then I seen Moon, standing still as a deer in the meadow, looking straight at me. You know how I am—

I reached for the licorice jar. 'How about that boy of yours?' I asked. 'Mind if I give him a licorice strap?'

"Paddie snorted, 'Him?' he said. 'I wish ye luck, tryin' to get him inside!'

"I didn't like him talking about his son like that. 'I believe I can walk,' I said, tartlike. So I took the licorice, started across the meadow. Moon, he hightailed it, always just out of reach, for all the world like some wild critter. So I laid the licorice down on that big rock, out there in the middle of the meadow, and went back to the store. Figured if he wanted it, he could get it.''

Olinger shook the dottle out of his pipe, swept both it and the charred wood into his hand, raised the stove lid, and emptied the blackened bits into the firebox. He wiped his hand on his trousers, and poured himself a cup of coffee. "Want some?" he asked. Harper shook his head. He wanted to hear the rest of the story.

"Anyway, I got back inside. 'What's his name?' I asked Paddie.

" 'Him? Aw, we call him Moon.'

" 'Seems like a peculiar name,' I said.

" 'Name's James. Not that he'd ever tell ye. Don't say two words a day, he don't. And when he does say somethin', ye can't understand him. A regular dumb bunny, he is! So I call him Moon, like that fellow Moon Mullins in the funny papers. Good for nothin's, the both of 'em, if ye ask me. . . .' ''

Olinger looked straight at Harper. "Can you beat that? A parent talking about his own son that way? I couldn't get over it. Anyway, the next thing I knew, there was

Moon, standing in the doorway. He'd wrapped that licorice around his head, weaving it in with the grass stems
and feathers, like some sort of crown." Olinger shook his
head. "My, he was a sight! His daddy wasn't too pleased.

"Paddie had growled, 'Now, ain't that somethin'! Give
the boy candy, he don't even know what to do with it.'
He'd turned to Moon. 'What'd ye say to the man?'

" 'For God's sake!' I said to Paddie. 'He don't have to
say nothing! You were a kid yourself, once. . . .' "

Olinger got up, added wood to the fire, rattled the grates
to shake down the ashes. "Paddie struck out for Walla
Walla a few minutes later. I watched him go. Couldn't see
Tessie—she must have been riding in back, same as always. Moon—he was clinging like a cat to the back of the
truck—wouldn't ride inside, even then. He waved at me."

Olinger stood up. "Let me show you something." He
reached up to the shelf that held the carvings, and felt
around. "Here it is." He sat down, holding a wreath of
some kind, with tiny stones and dried bits of grass and
flowers and feathers pressed into a round, dusty black
band.

"That day, I went back inside the store, and here was
that wreath he'd made, laying there like a gift. And I knew
he'd be back. And he has been, ever since, even when he
was just a little tyke, hiking that long road all alone. Stay-
ing for a while, then disappearing without a word."

There was a silence. Olinger chuckled. "How's that for
a long answer to a short question?"

He got up from the table and stirred the fire. "Tell you

what. How about if we hike down Bear Creek tomorrow, just the two of us? Catch ourselves a mess of trout."

"Sounds good."

"Then let's turn in. These few dishes can wait. We'll start by four-thirty or five in the morning, so's to get there when the fish are biting."

Ten minutes later, lying in his sleeping bag, listening to the night sounds—a rustling in the undergrowth, the far-off mournful yip-yip-yipping of a coyote, the hushed murmuring of the firs, the steady pat-a-pat of needles dropping onto the tent roof—Harper worked his way back over Olinger's conversation. Wasn't it strange, what a mystery a person's life could be? What else, he wondered, was there to know? What else?

5

Bear Creek

It was still dark outside when they left the cabin, but the sky to the east was that pale melon green that early morning brings. They'd eaten a hurried breakfast by lamplight: cold biscuits smeared with bacon grease, and warmed-up coffee.

Olinger had packed more biscuits and fried bacon in a bread wrapper for lunch and stuffed in a couple of candy bars. He broke down the fishing rods and tied the cotton strings around his oilskin packet of tackle. He laid his old pistol in the bottom of his creel. "Always take Old Bess along," he said. "You never know; one of these days she might come in handy."

As they were leaving he hung a hand-lettered sign on a nail outside the cabin.

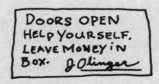

Half an hour later they stood at the rim of Bear Creek Canyon. In the dim light Harper could just make out the solemn ragged edge of firs on the far side. His boots were soaked through with morning dew, and his fingers tingled with the cold. Looking down into the hazy depths, he heard a deep, booming sound. He tried not to shiver. "That's Bear Creek you're hearing," Olinger said. "It's just a little bit of a thing, but it sure sounds loud by the time it's worked its way up out of there." He looked at Harper. "You cold?"

"A little." Harper hated to admit it.

"Sun'll be up in a few minutes, and the climb down's close to a mile—you'll warm up fast. So will the rattlers, so keep an eye out. They'll start to stir soon as the sun hits them."

It took over an hour—dropping hand over hand, sliding down outcroppings of shale, grabbing at huckleberry bushes and stunted pines, skirting clumps of poison oak— for them to reach the canyon floor. The slopes had been nearly bare of timber, except for the scraggly pines, but down here there were firs and tamaracks and an occasional locust and cottonwood, all so straight and tall that their trunks formed majestic columns, with a leafy canopy overhead. Ferns and tiny flowers grew in the dappled shade. Birds sang. Looking up, Harper could see golden sunlight moving down the high western wall of the canyon, but here the air was cool and damp.

The creek itself was tiny; so narrow that in many places one could jump across it. There'd be a pool, deep and still, then a jumble of boulders, and a plashing fall of three or four feet, and another pool.

Olinger dropped to his belly and began to drink. Harper joined him. The water was sweet and cold. Beneath his gaze he could see tiny grains of sand stirring and moving with the current.

Olinger took out his watch. "Quarter to six," he said. "We made good time." He started assembling his fly rod.

"You done much fishing?"

Harper nodded. "Some. With my dad. And Shorty."

"What'd you use?"

"Worms, mostly. Grasshoppers. Salmon eggs."

Olinger shook his head sadly. "Bait! I never could teach those boys anything important." He opened the little oilskin packet and selected a fly, a fluff of gray-and-brown feathers and red silk wrapped around a tiny hook. "That's a Royal Coachman. These trout, now, they think it's a mosquito or a gnat. Usually, they're pretty interested."

He rigged up Harper's rod and tied the tiny gray-and-brown fly to the leader. "I've cut the barbs off the hooks. That way, when we catch a trout, we can get the hook out without hurting the fish, usually. We throw back everything we catch, unless we hurt one bad; then we got to keep it. And we only get to keep six, the both of us. That's *my* rule, not the state's. So be careful. The easier we are with the fish, the longer we stay."

He showed Harper how to cast, whipping his line to keep the fly dry. "If that fly doesn't float, the trout's not interested. Now, let's give it a try."

On his first cast Harper had a strike. His heart leaped. He gave a hard yank and his hook and line sailed up behind him, catching high in a tree.

Olinger was at the next pool downstream, getting ready to cast. He grinned. "Forgot to mention that to you. See if you can wiggle it free. If you can't, you'll have to climb for it. . . . Whoops! Got one!" A glitter of silver sailed through the air. Olinger wetted his hands, gently removed the trout, and slid it back into the water, holding it for a second or two, then watching with pleasure as the fish swam away.

And so the morning went. Pool by pool, they worked their way down the little creek.

"How many you got?" Olinger asked after several hours had passed. Harper looked in his creel. "Four."

"And I just got my second one. That makes six. . . . You hungry?"

"You bet!"

Harper wolfed down his share of the biscuits and bacon, surprised at how small the portion seemed. The candy bar was gone almost as fast, and he was still hungry. Olinger filled the canteen, then nested the half dozen trout in a tangle of moss and damp grass and ferns in the bottom of Harper's creel. "We'll have those for supper," he said, "with fried potatoes and onions . . . *if* you've got your appetite back by then." He wiped the pistol dry with the bread wrapper and laid it back in his own creel.

They took one long, last drink from the creek.

"You about ready?" Olinger asked.

Harper had been dreaming of trout and fried potatoes. Now he remembered the loose shale and the rattlesnakes. His heart sank. "The same way we came?"

Olinger grinned and shook his head. "Nope. There's a trail somewhere around here. It's longer, but it sure beats fightin' shale."

For the first half hour they tramped easily through deep virgin forest, the trees towering overhead. Then the trail started uphill. For the next hour they hiked steadily. Harper could hear Olinger ahead of him, wheezing.

"What say we take a break," Olinger said, at the point of a switchback. Harper was gasping for breath. He nodded.

Olinger sat down on a rock. He opened the canteen and handed it to Harper. "Not too much, now," he cautioned. "Just a swallow or two. Let that settle. Then you can have more."

Harper lifted the canteen to his mouth, smelling its damp canvasy odor. He heard Olinger rummaging in his creel.

"Well, looky here!" Olinger said. "I plumb forgot I'd thrown in a couple of extra candy bars. You wouldn't be interested, would you?"

Harper couldn't remember anything ever tasting as good.

Then they were back on the trail again.

It was late afternoon by the time they reached the top. They crossed a barren meadow, with sharp rocks underfoot and stunted cheat grass moving stiffly in the afternoon breeze. Olinger was limping badly. "Durned knee!" he wheezed. "But it's not far now. We're less'n three miles from the cabin."

Harper, stumbling along, numb with fatigue, barely heard him.

Suddenly Olinger stopped.

"Listen!"

In the distance Harper could hear occasional whoops and shouting. "Somebody up ahead, where the timber starts again," Olinger whispered. "I can just barely see them. I don't know what they're up to, but I'd just as soon take it easy till we find out."

They stood for a moment, watching the distant figures. There were two of them, holding clubs, circling some object on the ground, occasionally giving a whack, shouting at each other, then circling again.

"I believe they've got somethin' caught in a trap," Olinger said. He looked at Harper. "We'll just mosey over, take a look. I don't like to raise trouble, but we may want a word or two with them."

As they drew nearer, Harper could see an animal crouched on the ground. The men were poised a few feet from it, clubs in the air.

"I believe it's a lynx," Olinger muttered. "See those ears, tufted up like that? And no tail to speak of?"

He was walking faster now, and the limp was nearly gone. He shouted a greeting. The men lowered their clubs and stood watching as Olinger and Harper approached. They were in their thirties, Harper guessed. One had a big belly hanging out where the pearl buttons on his fancy satin cowboy shirt had come unsnapped. Whiskers covered his whole face, so that only his eyes showed beneath his broken straw cowboy hat. The other was as lean as his companion was fat. He was wearing the same satiny shirt, greasy with wear. He had a long, doleful face and a scraggly mustache.

"Looks like you boys're having a little sport," Olinger said mildly.

The big-bellied one grunted. "Yep. Came up and set this trap last week, just for fun. I figgered we'd catch us somethin'. And look what we got! A bobcat! And boy, is he tough! Jeeter—he's my buddy, here—he got in a good lick, a few minutes ago. Stretched that cat out cold. But he was right back at us. Tough as nails."

"He's a goner, though, for sure, with me and Buck poundin' on him," Jeeter added, grinning, showing a gap where both front teeth were missing. "We don't give up."

"Don't seem like much of a contest," Olinger said.

"What'd you mean?"

"Well," Olinger said mildly, "with him caught in a trap like that, and you boys footloose and all, I wouldn't say he's got an even chance." Olinger paused. "I guess you know, by the way, traps like that are illegal."

There was a silence, broken only by the harsh panting of the bobcat.

"You aimin' to do something about it, Gramps?" the one named Buck asked.

Olinger shrugged. "I don't want to. But I might." He looked back at Harper. "Me and my partner, here."

Harper could feel his legs trembling.

"Oh, my!" Jeeter said, his voice high and mincing.

"You've got me soooo scared!" He raised his club. "Now, I don't want to hit an old man and a kid, but I believe if I was you, I'd just get the hell out of here, pretend you'd never seen us."

Olinger sighed. "I was afraid you were going to say something like that. Now, let me make a counter proposition. You two just skedaddle back to your truck, wherever you left it, and me and my partner'll take care of this cat."

"Why, you dumb old fart!" Buck thrust out his belly and took a couple of steps forward, raising his club in the air. "What you need is a little tap on the head to knock some sense in you."

"Now, boys," Olinger said, reaching into his creel and drawing out the pistol, "I'm reluctant to have to do this. In the first place, I'm no shot. And this old pistol here's not worth a tinker's dam. Aim for a foot—why, it's just as apt to hit somethin' bigger, like that belly of yours. And that'd be too bad. So, why don't you just line up with your backs to me, nice and straight, and see how far you can toss those clubs there into the undergrowth."

Buck and Jeeter growled, but they did what Olinger said.

"That's better. Now, you boys need to take those pretty shirts off."

"What for?"

"Why, to throw over the bobcat, while you spring that trap," Olinger explained as patiently as if he were giving Harper a lesson in fly casting. "I'll be durned if I want to see either of you get yourselves all scratched up. . . . It just wouldn't do. Now hurry it up. We don't have all day."

"Aw, we was just havin' a little fun!" Buck said. "Shoot, I wouldn't 'a hurt either one of you."

"That's fine, that's fine," Olinger said. "And I understand you changin' your tune. But now we've got this problem of this here bobcat stuck in a trap, and it's up to you two to get it loose. And we're just tryin' to help." He waved the pistol. "Get those shirts off."

Grumbling, they did so. Buck had a flag tattooed on his pale chest, with the script GOD BLESS AMERICA below it. A long red knife scar crossed Jeeter's abdomen.

"Now when I say go, give those shirts a fling over that cat's head and paws. You"—he motioned to Jeeter—"you grab that cat, hold him tight, while Big Belly there springs the trap. You'll have to move fast, the both of you, whilst he's tangled up like that. And remember, this had better work. You lose those shirts, you'll be doing it with your pants next time. You ready?"

Their faces grim, the two men nodded. They lifted their shirts. The bobcat snarled, shifting its gaze from side to side.

"Go!"

They dropped to their knees, throwing their shirts at the same time. Jeeter clutched frantically at the bobcat, trapped momentarily in the shirt, its powerful legs and claws straining against the fabric. Buck struggled with the rusty steel jaws of the trap. "Hold him, man! Hold him!" he shouted in a panic, coughing from the dust.

"He's tearing through!" Jeeter squealed. "He got my arm! Hurry it up, for God's sake! Oh! He got me again!"

"Got it! Let him loose!"

There was a whirl of fur and red shiny cloth, and the bobcat, shirts flapping behind it, took off, streaking through the trees. One shirt caught against a fallen branch and tore free. The other one snagged on a clump of poison oak.

The two men lay on the ground, gasping for breath. A line of blood oozed from Jeeter's arm.

"You did just fine, boys," Olinger said. "Now, if one of you'll free that trap and toss it over here to me, I'll see to it that it don't do any more harm—that's good. Harper, why don't you run fetch that shirt over there—the closest one—not the one in the poison oak. I believe we could use some bandages."

When Harper returned, Olinger was sitting on a fallen log, eyeing the two men. Jeeter was clutching his arm in an attempt to stop the blood. Buck was sprawled on his back, still breathing hard, his soft belly quivering with the effort. Olinger pulled the canteen free and tossed it toward the two men.

"Pour a little water on those scratches," he said. "And take a drink apiece, if you're thirsty. Then throw the canteen back to me, easy like. And, Mr. Belly, you bandage up your partner, there."

The men both drank, water running down their chins; then Buck sullenly began wrapping strips of fabric around Jeeter's arm.

"That should do it," Olinger said, watching. "Now, pull off your boots and stuff your socks inside. Then throw them out here to my partner."

"Criminy nettles, man!" Jeeter whined. "Give us a break!"

"I intend to. A sight better one than you were giving that cat. Now hurry it up. We don't have all day—Harper, pack one pair of boots up to the top of the meadow, and the other down there, toward the bottom. That way both these fellows'll get themselves a little exercise."

When Harper returned, Buck and Jeeter were on their feet, facing Olinger, who was sitting nonchalantly on the log, puffing on his pipe, the pistol lying in his lap.

"You boys about ready?"

"You crazy old coot!" Buck shouted. His face was livid. "You'll pay for this."

Olinger ignored him. "While you're waltzin' your way across those rocks," he said mildly, "you might want to meditate on how that bobcat felt, stuck there with a couple of bullies pounding away on him. Now start walking. And don't look back, or you might get me confused and I'd have to fire off a shot or two, just to clear my mind."

He picked up the trap and nodded to Harper. "Come on, partner. Let's go cook those trout!"

6

News from the Mountain

The next morning, while Harper and Olinger were finishing breakfast, they heard a car door slam, and then a shout. "It's my dad!" Harper said. He hurried outside. The morning mist was lifting from the meadow. Bushtits scolded each other in the wild roses. Dew rimmed the skunk cabbage leaves. The air had a crisp edge he'd not noticed before. Fall was on its way.

He hugged his father, smelling the familiar smells of sweat and pipe tobacco and freshly washed cotton shirting. Shorty cuffed him on his shoulder. "Danged young cub! Believe you've grown six inches!"

Olinger was standing in the doorway. "Well, look who's here! Come on in. I'll stir up a batch of pancakes."

Walter shook his head. "I wish we could, but we'd better not take the time. The prunes are coloring up fast, and the crew's starting to arrive. Whitey and Scotty came in yesterday; I expect the Keelings'll be here this afternoon. I hate like the dickens to show up early like this and spoil the party, but there's ladders to get out, and boxes, and picking sacks to mend—we could sure use some help."

Harper felt Olinger's callused old hand resting on his shoulder. "Well, we had a pretty good time, didn't we, son? Quiet, you understand. No real excitement—but now listen! You've got time for a cup of coffee, at least. I'll make up a fresh pot while Harper strikes his tent."

Half an hour later, they were ready to leave. A flat, shiny square under the big fir by the front of the cabin was the only thing remaining to show where the tent had been. The men shook hands. Olinger handed Walter a jar of fresh huckleberries for Jewel. Walter said they'd be sure to get back up, maybe even stay overnight, just as soon as the prunes were picked. And they'd bring Jewel too, that was a promise! They'd have a good time! Harper started to shake Olinger's hand, then, instead, threw his arms around him. He felt Olinger's stubbly cheek brushing against his. "Take care of yourself, partner," Olinger said gruffly. "Don't do anything I wouldn't do."

Harper tried to answer, but couldn't. It wasn't until the car pulled away that he could find his voice. "Good-bye, Olinger! Good-bye!" he shouted. "See you soon!"

But things didn't work out that way. Three days later, the prune season was in full swing. August passed. School started. As soon as the prunes ended, the apples were ready. September, then October hurried by. And then the first of the big storms arrived. The valley got rain, but up in the mountains there was snow—close to two feet, it was reported. "Biggest danged storm I can remember, this time of year," Shorty grunted.

"It doesn't look like we'll be seeing Olinger again until spring," Walter said. "Unless he takes a notion to hike out. I've known him to do that, once or twice."

The weather turned sunny and bright. Temperatures climbed back up to the low sixties. The men started fall pruning. One Saturday, a week after the big storm, Walter sent Shorty to town to buy nails and a roll of barbed wire, while he and Harper cleared fence rows and burned weeds in the big bare orchard. The sweet melancholy smell of smoke hovered in the golden air. To the west one could catch glimpses of the brown folds of the Horse Heaven Hills. Far to the east and south stretched the Blue Mountains, purplish and dreamy, crowned with snow. While he raked up lamb's-quarter and Russian thistles, Harper pictured Olinger up at the cabin, snug by the black kitchen stove, whittling away. Or maybe strapping on snowshoes to take a hike out to the Point.

"Any trouble finding barbed wire?" Walter asked Shorty that evening at the supper table.

Shorty was cutting his meat loaf into little bites. He shook his head. "Brinker'd saved some back for us. Had staples too, so I picked us up five pounds, just to be on the safe side. Heard an interesting story while I was there."

"What?" Harper asked.

Shorty shook ketchup onto his meat loaf and spooned a dollop of horseradish alongside. "Ah," he said, "just what the doctor ordered." He took a bite. His eyes watered. He coughed and sputtered. "Now," he said, wiping his mouth with his napkin, "that's what I call good!"

"What'd you *hear?*" Harper asked again.

Shorty poured coffee into his saucer, sipped, then picked up his fork and knife again. "Dave Titman and another feller just got down from the mountain. They said they was by Olinger's place last week."

"You mean after the big storm?" Walter asked. "How'd they manage that?"

"They was on snowshoes. They'd been huntin' for elk. Never had a bit of luck. Anyway, they was close by Olinger's store, so they stopped in to see how he was gettin' on."

"How was he?" Harper asked. Shorty could drag out a story longer than anyone he knew.

"That's the peculiar thing," Shorty said. He took a bite of meat loaf and chewed it slowly. "He wasn't there."

"You mean they couldn't find him?"

"That's right. They even snowshoed out to the Point. Not a sign of him, hide nor hair. Wasn't even tracks to the outhouse."

"Where'd they think he'd gone?" Jewel asked.

"Didn't have the faintest idea."

Harper tried to swallow, but couldn't. He'd never told Walter and Shorty about the bobcat, and Buck's blustering threats. ". . . I'd just as soon you not mention anything to your parents about our little run-in this afternoon," Olinger had said that last evening, during supper. ". . . you know how folks can get worked up. . . ."

"But maybe somebody shot him or something!" he said now.

Shorty snorted. "Olinger? Not that old geezer. He's too tough. My opinion is, he took off for Portland or somewhere on a toot. Prob'ly left before the storm hit. That'd account for no tracks."

Walter shook his head, puzzled. "I don't know. Somehow, that doesn't seem quite like him."

"What about the store?" Harper asked. "Was anything gone?" He was seeing Buck's face, livid with rage.

"Nothin' more'n you'd expect. That big quilt of his was gone from the bed, Dave said, but it stands to reason, the kind of weather they're havin' up there, if somebody was to come by, maybe on horseback, and offer him a ride, or he was to decide to hike out, he'd have taken that quilt with him to keep warm. Other'n that, though, the place was all tidied up, same as always—I never seen a man so cussed neat as Olinger. Dave did say he'd left a spoon, or a knife, in the sink. And a few shavings on the table, where he'd started another of his carvings. I don't know. Maybe he's improvin'."

Shorty tipped the meat loaf platter to drain a little juice onto his plate.

". . . No, the way I look at it, old Olinger's off having hisself a time. Remember how he done the same thing twenty years ago, not long after he'd come back from the army with that Bronze Star he got for wiping out a German machine-gun nest, and never even showin' us the medal? Gone for two months, and nary a word. Then one day in March we got that postcard from him, written all backwards, right to left, like he does sometimes, almost like a code, and a week later, here he come draggin' in, so shaky he couldn't drink a cup of coffee without spillin' it. Not a word about what he'd been up to. Went right back up the mountain, opened the store up, same as if he'd never been away."

"You mean Olinger's a hero?"

"About as genuine as you can get," Shorty said. "Ask your dad."

Walter nodded. "It's true, although you'd sure never worm it out of him. Only way we found out was when the newspaper carried a story. Did it single-handed, to save his squad. . . . still and all, that was a long time ago. Olinger's pushing sixty-five, if he's a day. It just doesn't seem likely a fellow his age would go chasing off at the drop of a hat."

"Was there a note or anything?" Jewel asked.

"Nope. Not that Dave could find."

"Maybe somebody murdered him for his money," Harper said. He wished he could tell them about Buck and Jeeter.

His father shook his head and gave a fond chuckle. "They'd sure be wasting their time. He'd rather give you something than sell it to you. Especially kids." Walter turned to Shorty. "What about the money, though? Did Dave say anything?"

Shorty shook a little more ketchup onto his plate. "Everything was right there in the cash box, the bills with rubber bands tied around 'em like always. Dave counted it; said they was nearly a hundred dollars. Even some small change."

"It seems peculiar that he'd not take the money with him if he was going off for the winter," Walter said.

Shorty shook his head. "Not the way I look at it. If he's headin' off on a spree, what he don't have, he won't spend. So he takes a few bucks—dollar bills—but don't touch the big stuff: tens and twenties. That'd be one way of keepin' hisself out of trouble."

Jewel picked at some crumbs that had fallen onto the tablecloth and arranged them in a little pattern on her plate. "Is there anyone else up there who might know where he's gone?"

Shorty shook his head. "Nope. That mountain's cleaned out of people this time of year. There was that old coot lived by hisself, up there near Tollgate. What the heck was his name? Zedler Cupples, that's it! But he's been dead for more'n a year now."

They were all silent. Walter sopped up the last bit of meat juice on his plate with a corner of bread, then turned to Jewel. "I believe that's the finest meal you ever cooked," he said.

Shorty broke in. "Say, I plumb forgot the other news. Moon's joined the army."

"Moon?" Harper couldn't believe it. And without saying good-bye! Moon wouldn't do that!

"When did that happen?" Jewel said.

"Last week or so. Brinker seen his name printed up in the paper, along with some other Freewater boys that

joined up the same time. Showed it to me. I didn't recognize his name at first—James Patrick McCarty—same
as his daddy's. But they'd stuck his other name alongside,
so's people'd know who he was, I guess."

Walter grunted. "Well, I sure hope the army knows what
it's getting into, trying to make a soldier out of him."

"What makes you say that?" Jewel asked.

"Now, Jewel," Walter said, "don't get in a huff. I know
you've always had a soft spot for him; poor motherless
chick. And I don't blame you. But you never tried to get
any work out of him, like I have. It's like trying to lasso
a butterfly. And I doubt that he's had a year of schooling
in his life."

"There's lots of things he can do," Harper said. "He
knows about wild things. Maybe even how to talk to them.
And he can make anything."

Shorty nodded. "Harper's sure right about that," he
said to Walter. "Give Moon a few sticks or some feathers
or a little stove wire—anything; and he'll make somethin'.
And not just somethin' dumb, either. I mean somethin'—
well—just plain beautiful."

"He got some of that from his father," Walter agreed.
"I've seen Paddie paint peaches you swear you could eat."

"And tough!" Shorty said. "Why, I run across him a
year ago, halfway out to Starbuck, lopin' along the road
in that funny, easy way of his. And get this: He was plan-
nin' on startin' back that same day! Why, there and back
must be close to a hundred miles! When Moon gets it into
his head to go somewhere—day, night—they're both the
same to him. No. Harper's right. Moon's got talent. If

the army could just get him to show up when they want him, they'd have themselves one fine doughboy."

"I wish them luck," said Walter. "I have a feeling they're going to need it."

Jewel sighed and rose from the table, went to the kitchen counter, and returned with a pie. "Apple," she said. ". . . I'm just surprised that he didn't drop by to tell us he was leaving. And disappointed too, I guess. Somehow, it's always seemed to me that, in a way, we're his family."

Walter nodded absently. "I know, I know." He looked out the window at the darkness. "I just wish I didn't feel so uneasy about Olinger," he said.

"How about going up there?" Harper suggested, not wanting to sound too eager.

"It's a possibility. We might get the truck up a good share of the way, if we put on chains. Then hike on in."

"When?" Harper asked. "Tomorrow?"

Walter shook his head. "Not tomorrow. I promised your Uncle Dale we'd help shingle his woodshed in the afternoon. And we're tied up the first part of the week too. But maybe next Saturday. That way you could ride along, if you wanted."

Harper didn't answer.

"Now, Jewel," Walter said, "I believe I'll have a piece of that pie, before these two try to steal my share."

While the others listened to the evening news on the radio, Harper washed the dishes, going over the whole conversation again. Something had happened to Olinger; he was sure of it. And his father wasn't going to do anything about it for a week! Why, that was crazy! If Moon was here, he knew what Moon would do—Moon would start up the mountain tomorrow morning. Or maybe even tonight!

He started to dry the plates, stacking them in the pantry. But Moon wasn't here. Going off to the army, and not even coming by to say he was leaving? That didn't make any sense! None of it made any sense.

Later, Shorty challenged him to a game of checkers. Harper lost. They played another game. Harper lost again.

Shorty got to his feet and hobbled to the door, whistling for his dog, Bob. "I don't know what's got into you, boy," he said to Harper, "but if the way you play checkers is any indication, I believe there's somethin' sappin' your mind."

A few minutes later Harper said good night and climbed the stairs up to his bedroom. He undressed, the linoleum floor like ice beneath his bare feet. Olinger needed him. He knew he did. Not next week. Right now!

He scrambled into his pajamas and crawled into bed, drawing the heavy quilts up to his nose.

How far was it up to Olinger's? Twenty, twenty-five miles? Bet he could ride his bike up there and back in a day. Except for the snow. But with these last weeks of warm weather, there'd only be snow the last few miles. He could ride his bike the first part of the way.

Far off he could hear the mournful whistle of the night train, climbing the grade up from the Columbia River. When could he go? Tomorrow. No. Not tomorrow. If he went tomorrow, they'd know he was gone. Monday. Yes. Monday. When everyone thought he was off to school. That's when he'd go. Monday.

7

A Light in the Window

By eight o'clock Monday morning, pedaling hard, Harper was passing through the little town of Freewater, on his way up to Olinger's.

He'd left the house earlier than usual that morning, lamely explaining to his mother that he'd promised to help Mrs. Emory, his teacher, clean out the supply room. ". . . And I may have to stay after school too if we don't finish," he'd added. Jewel was busy with the Monday wash and had nodded her consent.

A couple of pickup trucks were parked outside the Tee-pee Tavern, and spilling out the open door came men's talk, and a waitress's laugh, and the smoky smells of hot-cakes and ham and potatoes and onions frying. The radio was playing "The White Cliffs of Dover." For the first time since starting out, his determination wavered. Why wasn't he home where he belonged, practicing his piano lesson, finishing his arithmetic, getting ready for school?

But then the sun broke over the foothills, and a cat

scooted across the road with a dog chasing it, barking wildly. He crossed the Walla Walla River bridge, the frost-whitened planks thumping under his tires. A mud-spattered truck passed him, going the other way, the driver waving a cheery greeting. Harper ducked his head so his face wouldn't show and kept on pedaling. No sirree! he told himself. He was going up to Olinger's like he'd planned. That was that!

The valley was narrowing rapidly now. A few dreary little houses hugged the road. Chickens scratched for bugs in the straggly lanes leading back to weathered packing sheds, half hidden by bare-branched orchards. Pumpkins and squash, tethered to frosted vines, squatted in the corn-fields. Cattle grazed in stony meadows. A flock of crows reproached him from a cottonwood tree. Ahead, he saw the turnoff for Lincton Mountain. From there on, the road was dirt.

But he'd already come close to ten miles. Why, he was practically halfway to Olinger's, and it probably wasn't much past nine o'clock. And here his father and Shorty weren't sure they could make the trip!

When he reached the turnoff Harper climbed off his bike and stood for a moment looking back at the valley and the brown fallow hills stretching off to the west. To the east the mountain appeared to be one long gentle slope, with great fields of wheat stubble stretching across its face, and canyons, purple and hazy in the thin sunlight, creasing its expanse. At the very top of the slope, he could make out the first pines. That's where the snow waited, if there was snow. Maybe there wouldn't be any; maybe he'd be able to ride his bike all the way to the cabin. Wouldn't Olinger be surprised?

The road was starting to climb now, and he stood on the pedals and pumped, feeling the sweat under his heavy mackinaw. Ahead, too late to avoid it, he saw a slick of yellow clay. He swerved, his rear tire started to slide, and he pitched forward, sprawling across the handlebars.

Dazed, he scrambled to his feet, wiping the clay from his face and spitting gravel from his mouth, and stood for a minute, trembling. He'd scratched his cheek, and his right hand stung where he'd slammed it against an out-cropping of rock, but he could wiggle his fingers. Nothing broken.

He picked up his bike, climbed on, and gave a shove. The front tire rubbed against the fork. Darn! The wheel must be bent.

Laying the bike down, he jammed a rock on either side of the bent place, and pushed down on the wheel with his foot. There! That ought to fix it. He gave the wheel a spin. It still rubbed, a squeaky, repeating sound; scree, scree, scree . . . He tried again, but no luck.

Now what? He looked west, feeling the cold breeze on his face, trying to find a good answer. Far off, down in the valley, he could hear the faint, friendly sputter and cough of a tractor, but that was all, except for the lonesome whisper of the wind blowing across the sparse dried cheat grass. Somehow, he hadn't counted on it being so empty up here.

Well, he'd just have to hike the rest of the way. Oh, it might take a little longer. Four or five hours instead of two or three. But Olinger was sure to be back from wherever he'd gone. They'd spend an hour or so, have a bite to eat. Why, he'd be back here by five in the afternoon. He could probably catch a ride home from the main road. He'd be home by six o'clock at the latest.

On the other hand, maybe this was a sign. If he turned around right now and headed for school, he'd be there in time for lunch. He could make up something to tell Mrs. Emory—Jewel thought he was coming down with a cold. No one would need to know what he'd tried to do.

Maybe that made more sense. Probably the men would be coming up later this week; they'd surely take him along. And if Olinger was safe—and of course he was—would he appreciate some kid hooking school to check up on him like he was some sort of invalid? No. The best thing was to head back now, before it got too late. No one could say he hadn't tried.

Feeling a sense of relief, he reached for his lunch sack and sat down on a boulder, gazing about. He'd just eat one of his sandwiches before starting back; he could save the other one for when he got to school.

The sky was freshly washed, clear and blue—almost the color of summer—but thinner, somehow, with that diminished light fall brings. The air was cold. A hawk soared into view, its wing tips canted to better catch the wind, swinging ever higher in a slow, graceful arc.

What if Olinger was hurt and needed him?

Now, why did he have to go and spoil everything, thinking that way? Why, Olinger knew the woods like the back of his hand. No way would he get himself in a jam he couldn't work his way out of.

Harper finished his sandwich, licked his fingers, and considered eating the second one as well. No. He'd better wait until he got back to school. That's where he was going, wasn't it? It'd look suspicious if he didn't have his lunch.

Well, what *would* he have found, just supposing he had gone on up the mountain? He picked at a lichen on the rock, vaguely admiring the soft gray and mustard colors, the crenulated fringes.

What about Buck and Jeeter? What if they'd carried out their threats?

Darn it! There he was—doing it again, thinking about Olinger! Why, Olinger didn't have an enemy in the world, except, maybe, for Buck and Jeeter. And they were just a couple of two-bit creeps. Besides, Dave Titman said there was close to a hundred dollars in the cash box, and it hadn't been touched. Surely, if Buck and Jeeter had been there, they wouldn't have left the money behind.

He wiped the bit of lichen from his fingers and unwrapped his second sandwich. Guess he'd eat it now. If he did go back to school today, he could tell them he'd had lunch at home. When the sandwich was gone, he pulled out his apple and took a bite. No use carrying all that extra baggage.

When he'd finished the apple, he stuffed his empty lunch sack behind the boulder and pulled a tumbleweed over his bike for cover. He sniffed and wiped his nose with his finger, then pulled his mittens back on. He took a look back down the way he'd come. Then, to his own surprise, he started up the road toward Olinger's.

"Okay," he muttered aloud, talking to the earth, to the sky, "now what do you say?"

An hour later he paused, out of breath, to rest. There'd been snow here, although the sun had melted most of it, leaving only a thin white rime under the lee of rocky outcroppings. The wind was picking up, but he wasn't cold. The brisk pace he'd set took care of that. He glanced at the sky. High above, long horsetail clouds swept past. Hope that didn't mean another storm.

Ahead was the first dark line of trees. They looked forbidding, and he felt a brief sense of panic. "Stop that," he muttered to himself. "They're just trees, that's all. Nothing to be afraid of."

His right sock had worked its way down inside his boot, and he could feel the beginnings of a blister. He found a rock and sat down, unlaced his boot and examined the red spot on his heel, touching it gingerly. Too bad he didn't have some tape. Maybe if he pulled the sock up and rolled it over the top of the boot, that would keep it from rubbing.

He relaced his boot and started out again. Suddenly, for the first time that morning, he was in deep shadow, surrounded by the rich pungent smell of pine. Snow crunched underfoot. He shivered, astonished at the sudden cold, here in the shade. Then, just as suddenly, he was in the welcome sunlight again, beyond the first clump of trees, and the snow was gone, except for a thin drift nestled against the bank of the road. Then shadow again.

The forest was closing in fast now; dark and ominous, and the road was growing narrower and narrower. Even when there was a bit of open country, he was picking his way around drifts, and where the road was bare, the mud looked like frozen chocolate, edged with frost.

Another drift, and then another, and then, ahead of him, not more than thirty yards away, he saw the road disappear entirely under a covering of snow. He floundered on, watching where he was stepping, trying to avoid the deeper drifts. The sock had worked its way down into his boot again, rubbing against his heel and bunching up under his instep. And he was thirsty.

A crow cawed. Glancing up, Harper saw something moving silently through the forest ahead of him, but it drifted away even as he watched. He stumbled on, trying to remember where he'd seen it. There? Or was it further on, past that dead snag? He stopped and listened. Silence, except for the eerie whisper of wind in the top branches of the dark trees.

Maybe it was a mountain lion. He felt the sweat break out on his body.

Come on now. How many times had he ever heard of someone being attacked by a panther? Never. But there was always a first time.

Now he thought he sensed a movement behind him. He glanced back, feeling the hair on his neck bristling. Hah! A chipmunk, scurrying up a tree! But that wasn't what he'd seen before.

The snow was halfway up to his knees now. His shirt was wet with sweat under his mackinaw, his legs were tired, and he could feel the blister puffing up on his heel. His boots were wet clear through, and his sock was bunched in a ball under his instep. And suddenly he had to pee. And the light was changing; growing darker, bluer; it must be after one in the afternoon, and getting colder; the wind flinging granules of snow, thin and hard as sand, in his face.

But he recognized ahead of him the thicket of wild plums, and the spinney of wild brambles, frosted with snow, and the huge old dead pine. Just a couple of hundred more yards, if he remembered correctly. And look, a broken-down barbed-wire fence. Bet that's what he'd seen—a stray cow some rancher had left behind. No, there wasn't a cow alive that could drift away like what he'd seen, silent as a ghost. Could just be a deer, though.

Then, around the bend, he saw the opening in the forest, and sensed, even though he could not see it, the vast canyon off to the left, where the Walla Walla River ran dark and full and swift. He was hurrying now, squinting against the glare of snow to catch his first sight of Olinger's store, hunkered down safe and snug in its little snowy meadow, with the pines and firs standing guard around it.

There! There it was! And look! A light in the window! His heart flip-flopped with relief. Olinger! Olinger was safe! What a story he'd have to tell them when he got back home!

8

Olinger Shows Up

Across the meadow stood the silent cabin, a foot of snow blanketing its roof, its window ablaze with light. But wait! That wasn't lamplight. It was a chance ray of afternoon sunlight, reflecting off the windowpane.

A breeze stirred the dark firs, so that they whispered mournfully. Harper's terror returned. His legs were trembling, and his fingers and toes were aching with the cold, and the sock in his right boot felt hard as an anvil. He groaned. Why wasn't he at school; bored, safe, diagramming sentences, memorizing continents and countries, instead of up here, freezing to death, fighting back terror, pretending to be a hero?—and all the time stuck with the nagging feeling that something, someone, was behind him, worrying him like a sheepdog, edging him closer and closer to Olinger's cabin.

Cut it out! he told himself. You're imagining things! Besides, he'd done what he'd set out to do, hadn't he? And see? Olinger had just gone off somewhere, like

Shorty'd said. That settled it. No use wasting time poking around. He'd pull up his socks and head back home.

But first, no matter what happened, he had to pee.

He unbuttoned his trousers and for a long, blissful moment stood watching the steam rise as he wrote his name in the snow, making it all the way to the last *r* before he ran out.

Shaking the last drops free, he sneaked a quick look behind him. No one. Maybe he'd been wrong. He sure hoped so.

He buttoned his pants, and he put his mittens on, then studied the sky, looking nonchalant for an audience that he was practically certain didn't exist.

He tried taking a step or two back the way he'd come, looking for a rock, a tree stump, to sit down on, so he could pull his socks up. But whatever had been nudging him forward all morning wasn't about to let go now.

"All right, all right!" he grumbled aloud, in case someone was listening. "I guess it wouldn't hurt to take a look inside—find a dry pair of socks before I start back."

Warily, his breath coming fast, he limped across the meadow. The thick, leathery brown leaves of an occasional skunk cabbage, pointed like the ears of a buried animal, showed here and there above the snow. Suddenly his heart leaped with fright. What was this? Snowshoe prints; two sets of them, coming from the other direction and heading toward the cabin!

Calm down, calm down, he told himself, trying to catch his breath. Those were Dave Titman's tracks; Dave's and his partner's. See? They stopped here, at the cabin door. They'd taken their snowshoes off and poked them in the snow before going inside. And see? Here's where they'd started out toward the Point, and come back, and then rejoined the trail they'd made on the way in. He felt a little smug with his detective work. And comforted to know that someone else had been here. And gone.

He tried the latch and pushed at the door. It stuck. He pushed again; the hinges creaked, and the old planks gave under his hand. The familiar, friendly Olinger smells of last summer reached out: apples and tobacco smoke, sweat, bacon and tar and old boots and rubber. Kerosene. Wood smoke. Mice. All the same. But different, somehow; the smells of an abandoned cabin, the smells of disuse and loneliness.

For a few seconds he stood peering into the cold, dim interior, his eyes adjusting to the darkness: seeing the table with its oilcloth covering and ketchup bottle and salt and pepper shakers where he and Olinger had shared so many happy meals; the tin sink and galvanized bucket; the cook stove; the wood box; the bed in the corner; the coats and skis and snowshoes and caps hanging on their pegs; the worn leather chest; Olinger's carvings on their high shelf; the back wall, with its meager shelves of canned goods; the store counter.

Someone was hiding behind the counter—he was sure of it.

He crept across the worn board floor and peered around. Nothing, except for some empty candy boxes and a few bird feathers piled together. Something rustled, and he jumped. But it was just a mouse, scurrying to the wood box.

He continued his search. What was this? A knife in the sink. He started to pick it up, then stopped short. What would Dick Tracy do? Save the fingerprints, for sure. Wrapping the dishrag around the knife handle, he held it up so the blade could catch the light entering from the tiny window over the sink. What was that dark brown stain? Blood?

He groaned. He wasn't cut out to be a detective. Lying in his own bed, at home, answers to questions like these came easily. But here in Olinger's cabin, with his nose dripping, and his sock bunched worse than ever under his foot, and somebody probably outside sneaking up on the cabin at this very instant, how could he hope to figure out anything?

With shaking hands, he scratched the stain with a fingernail, then lifted the knife to his nose.

Beans! Van Camp's pork and beans. He'd know the smell anywhere. Olinger's favorite. Relief flooded through him. He'd solved the Mystery of the Bloodstained Knife. Here he was imagining murder, and all he was seeing was evidence of Olinger's last meal before he took off for Portland, or wherever he'd headed. Could even be Dave Titman had helped himself to a can of beans.

Feeling easier, he surveyed the cabin again. On the checkered oilcloth of the table was a piece of weather-stained pine. He picked it up; feeling the heft of it in his hand, seeing the rough shape of a blue jay, almost smiling. Olinger, starting another carving.

Setting the chunk of wood aside, he helped himself to a 3 Musketeers from one of the candy boxes, savoring the rich comforting smell of chocolate. The three chunks of candy were gone in an instant. He licked his fingers, started toward the door, then dug in his pocket for a nickel and put it in the box Olinger kept for making change. He wished he had enough money to buy another one. It sure had tasted good.

He peered out the open door. The blue in the sky had grown darker in the last few minutes, and horsetail clouds were catching light, high above. The air was getting colder all the time. He'd better start back before it got any later. Rummage up some socks and head for home.

But no, not yet. He couldn't go yet. He cocked his head, listening. For what? A voice, maybe, telling him what to do? No. Not a sound, other than the steady lonesome hum of the wind in the trees, and the faint gurgle of the spring. He scanned the area outside the cabin door, not sure what he was even looking for. Footprints? A sign— THIS WAY TO OLINGER—showing him the way? But all he could see was the dense growth of slender fir trees, standing as if in judgment of him.

He winced. "Okay, okay!" he muttered. He'd just take a quick look around out back. Then he'd borrow a pair of socks and start for home.

Pulling his cap down over his ears, he left the cabin, glancing cautiously around, then struck out down the path behind the cabin, jumping across the little murmuring spring, the snow banking sharply on either side, trying not to look back at every step.

Maybe he should stop and get a drink. He was terribly thirsty, and the candy had made it worse. He hesitated. But there was the nudge again. All right! All right! He'd wait till he was ready to start back. He struggled on, floundering now and then in the deep snow, trying to follow Dave Titman's tracks, until he reached the outhouse. He peered inside, seeing the smooth, worn plank seat and torn Sears catalog, smelling the faintly comforting human smells of urine and excrement.

There! He'd gone far enough. No sign of Olinger. And he'd done more than he needed to. He could go back to the cabin now, get a drink of water, fix his socks, and head for home. He'd be out of the snow in an hour. It'd be a lot faster going down. He wouldn't have to break trail, for one thing. And the road home always seemed shorter, he'd noticed that. He wondered what Jewel was fixing for supper. Maybe he could take another candy bar and pay Olinger next summer. That wouldn't be stealing, would it?

Yes. He'd start back now. He'd done what he set out to do.

But there came the nudge again. Reluctantly he moved away from the outhouse, hating to leave, missing already the friendly human stink of it. This way, this way, the nudge seemed to say, drawing him on, drawing him away from the familiar path leading to the Point, drawing him deeper and deeper into the forest. He was breaking trail now, floundering in the snow, cold through and through; his nose raw and stinging, his fingers stiff; his garments damp and chill, snow caking on his trousers well up past his knees.

The trees were close together here and nearly impenetrable, but he remembered a path leading through them. He and Moon had walked that path in the summertime, when the jack-in-the-pulpit was in bloom and the mosses were covered with white flowers no larger than a pinhead, when the wild strawberries gleamed like rubies, and the earth underfoot was soft and silent, when the fir needles were warm and fragrant with the filtered sun.

Now, though, the path was hidden under snow, and fallen needles fashioned patterns like Chinese writing on its pale blue surface. Ahead, through the trees, he saw an abandoned shed. He'd played Indians there, years ago, all by himself, on a warm, safe summer day, while the insects hummed, and the men sat in the sunshine back at the store, smoking and swapping stories. But now the roof shingles were gone, the rafter boards broken like matchsticks, and the bark was working loose from the cribbed poles, showing wood the color of ashes.

He ducked his head and peered into the gloom. Tiny drifts of snow dotted the musty hay. A fork with a broken handle had been shoved into the rotted hay; it stood there, erect as a marker. Harper reached to touch it, surprised at how smooth and oily the handle felt against his mittened hand. Hard to believe it hadn't been used for years.

And now, a thumping sound he'd not heard before—thump thump thump . . . Calm down, he told himself, it's your own heart you hear! Here in this narrow space, things sound different. In a panic, he left the shed, staggering through the snow, scrambling over a fallen tree, muttering to himself.

Suddenly he was falling, falling—sinking deep in the snow. He struggled, terrified, twisting his body, trying to get back on his feet, floundering in a welter of snow and branches and fir needles and old musty hay, helpless as an overturned beetle. Snow covered his face and eyes like frozen lace, and through the snow he saw the dark branches of the firs spinning a clumsy net overhead.

What was that?

There, in the snow, pushing against his leg, was the tip of an olive-colored gum boot, powdered snow clinging to its yellow sole. He shrank away, trying to move, shaking down more snow and more needles. Something shoved against his thigh. He saw the dark canvas lumberjack trousers, and the edge of a faded quilt.

Oh my God! Olinger wasn't in Portland, off on a toot. Olinger was lying here under his own quilt, half buried beneath a thatch of fir needles and snow.

He flailed at the snow, grabbing a huckleberry bush and pulling himself upright. Panting hard, he stood staring wildly at the shadows surrounding him. A chipmunk chirruped from a branch overhead, and the wind stirred the firs. And the thumping sounded more loudly than ever.

Wait a minute.

Something didn't make sense. Olinger wasn't really buried. Why, all he had was a quilt wrapped around him, and a few fir needles.

Suddenly, gratefully, Harper realized the happy truth. The thump, thump, thump he'd been hearing—that wasn't *his* heart; that was Olinger's. Olinger was alive. And he, Harper, was going to save him. He remembered cases he'd read, in Tibet, in Alaska, where people had drifted off, and the snow covered them, and they'd lain there for a week or a month—some of them for a year or so, and when they got free they were just as good as new. That's what had happened to Olinger! Maybe he'd had a little too much to drink and wandered out to look at the stars and fallen down, and . . .

Yes. That's what had happened. Of course! This wasn't a grave. There'd always been a little shallow spot here. Remember? Probably an old root cellar. Why, Olinger had stumbled in, just as he himself had stumbled, and passed out, and the snow had come, falling, soft as a blanket, and covered him, and he was still alive, and there hadn't been a murder, and he'd just wake Olinger up, and they'd go back to the store, and build a fire, and Olinger'd make coffee and heat up a can or two of Van Camp's pork and beans, and they'd laugh, and he'd tell Olinger about trying to steal a candy bar from him, and then not being able to, and leaving a nickel, and Olinger would laugh and slap him on the back, and call him partner, and give him a licorice strap, like he'd done ever since Harper could remember.

Why, he bet Olinger would want to head back down to the valley with him this evening. Now, wouldn't that be something! They'd come hiking in the lane, the two of them, and the lamps would be on, and Jewel would be in the kitchen, and they'd come up the steps, and pound on the front door, and Walter and Shorty would be at the supper table, and Olinger'd tell them all how Harper had saved his life, and Walter and Shorty would tell him he was a real hero. . . .

He was brushing the snow and fir needles away now, in his haste to get Olinger up so they could get going—the old man had probably been cold when he left the cabin, and he'd grabbed his quilt up. That explained the needles. He'd pulled those around himself to keep warm. Sure.

He tugged at the quilt, and snow cascaded down about him like great chunks of soft sugar. He shivered. Funny, but for a moment the quilt reminded him of a shroud, like something out of the Bible. But then reason returned. What about the thump, thumping? That was the old man's heart, wasn't it, sturdy as ever, pump, pumping away?

The quilt had gotten damp, and part of it was frozen stiff, but he was getting Olinger free. See? He was wearing his black-and-red checkered mackinaw, like he'd put on for going out in the woods. (My, just look how thin and drawn and pale his hands were, as if all the blood had been drained from them!)

He broke more snow away, eager to waken the old man. Wasn't he lucky? Why, it was like rousing someone from the dead. Reverend Wheeler would tell about it in church. Lazarus? Was that the guy in the Bible that Jesus had brought back to life? And there'd be a story in the *Walla Walla Union Bulletin:* LOCAL YOUTH FREES MOUNTAIN STORE OWNER FROM SNOWY GRAVE.

He was brushing Olinger's collar free, and his old neck,

withered and wrinkled as a turkey's. And his chin, with its stubble of whiskers . . . and the mouth, thin-lipped and gray . . . and the yellow wax of his cheeks . . .

Maybe they should stay the night in the cabin, build a fire, have supper, and start down in the morning. That might be a better idea. His parents would worry, but after they found out what had happened, they'd understand. After what Olinger'd been through, maybe it would be too much to expect him to make that long trip this late in the day.

Suddenly the entire crust of snow broke free from Olinger's face. His eyes were closed, the lids thin and dry. And what was this on his forehead? A sharp gash, the blood dried, the skin around it a queer, greenish color.

The jay scolded again, and off in the dense woods he heard a muffled sound of scurrying in the snow. Some small wild creature looking for shelter.

"Olinger!" he yelled. "Wake up! It's Harper!"

The old man didn't stir.

Harper grabbed his cheeks, feeling the cold, stiff, waxy skin, the whiskery stubble. "Olinger!" he pleaded. "It's me! Harper! Wake up!"

Frantically, his fingers full of hope, he lifted an eyelid, the membrane fragile as a bird's. Where the glistening blue should have been, the eye was a dull pale yellow. Without warning he tasted the hot sweet taste of vomit, and 3 Musketeers chocolate candy spewed all over Olinger's bright red-and-black mackinaw.

"Olinger! Oh, my God! No!"

9

Alone

Oh, my God! Oh, my God! Oh, my God! He was stumbling down the trail through the snow, gasping for air, his breath sawing against his chest. Ahead he saw the pale glistening light of the meadow. If he could get that far at least he'd be out in the open.

Something grabbed him by the leg. He tumbled in a heap, then scrambled to his feet and looked back. No one. He was out to the road now, the snow unbroken except for the trail he'd made on the way in. He sobbed, his breath catching in his throat. His chest heaved with effort. He could run no farther.

He turned.

The tall narrow firs stood as dark and unmoving as cemetery markers, with Olinger's tiny cabin squatting under them. Harper listened. A jay bird squawked, then was still. The wind vibrated against the rusty strands of a barbed wire fence, sticking up out of the snow. Far below, he heard the echoing lonely booming vastness of the river gorge. The sky was the hard deep sapphire blue of a winter evening, feathered with high clouds, tinged in the west with the faint orange of sunset. The silhouette of a hawk circled in the darkening air. Harper watched the distant speck for a moment, longing to match the bird's easy, motionless flight. If he were a bird, he'd be safe.

And then, even as he watched, he saw, or thought he saw, the hawk give a frantic lunge upward, then collapse and tumble through the sky toward the earth. Harper stared in disbelief and horror. What had he seen? One instant the bird was alive and serene, and the next it was nothing but a frantic handful of feathers, dying or already dead, falling like a dust bag through the sky.

Nonsense! He'd just imagined it. He'd imagined everything; the fleeting shadows, the hawk . . . But he hadn't imagined Olinger. Gasping, he shoved snow in his mouth to wash away the bitter taste of vomit, then wiped his face with snow, grateful for the harsh sting of ice on his skin. He heard his own deep, drawn-in breathing, and felt ashamed. He was too old to cry.

"Socks," he said aloud. He had to fix his socks. He couldn't go on until he pulled up his socks. Just as soon as he fixed his socks, he'd start down the mountain.

He looked back at the cabin. There'd be dry socks in the cabin. He could even build a fire.

No. That was a trick. He wasn't going back to the cabin, not for all the money in the world. Somebody—something—was back there. Something so clever it had left no track in the snow; waiting, just waiting, till it had driven him to the point where he was so exhausted and crazy he couldn't lift a finger. He looked up again at the heavens, where the hawk had soared, not two minutes ago. Already the moon was showing white. He'd see the first stars in less than an hour. And then, night would fall.

Suddenly he was terribly tired. His stomach felt shriveled and empty and sour, and his mouth burned from the snow. He was shaking uncontrollably with the cold; his teeth chattering against one another. He wasn't going to make it back down the mountain this evening, no matter how much he wanted to. Something had killed Olinger, and something had killed the hawk, and whatever it was that had killed them was stalking him as well. He could run or he could stand. Either way, he was caught.

He cupped his mittens up to his mouth. "Get lost!" he shouted. He waited.

". . . Lost," a voice echoed back, ". . . lost . . ."

He shouted again, his voice breaking. "I'm not afraid!"

". . . afraid . . . afraid . . . afraid . . ."

The echo taunted him.

No, by golly! He wasn't giving up. He'd sit down for a minute, fix his sock. Then he'd head out. Little dots danced in front of his eyes. His ears were ringing, a hard, steady steely sound.

He rubbed his mitten over his face, hands trembling. If he went back to the cabin, he could build a fire. If he built a fire, he could heat a can of beans. He imagined, briefly, the warm, slippery chunks of pale pork fat sliding down his throat, and the sweet, soft, grainy texture of syrupy brown beans. If he went back to the cabin, at least he'd not die hungry.

No. That was another trick.

He was going down the mountain. He'd outrun whatever it was that was following him.

But what if it was leading him? If it was leading him, how far could he outrun it? How far was it to the nearest house? Fifteen miles? And how far would he get before he simply couldn't walk any farther? He sniffled, then started to cry. He wiped his eyes. What a coward he was!

A sign—that's what he needed. He stood waiting for a sign; something—anything—telling him what to do. A bird's call. A star shooting across the heavens. The voice of an angel calling his name.

But no sign came. He read that for a sign, and took what seemed to him to be the coward's way out. Reluctantly, heart pounding, he started back toward the cabin. His eyes had puffed up so that he could barely see, and his nose was running a snotty stream. He wiped it, feeling the sting where he'd rubbed the skin raw.

He pushed open the door and nearly fell into the dark interior.

"Go ahead," he muttered. "You win."

He waited. Nothing happened.

"A fire. Got to get a fire going."

He shook the grates and adjusted the draft, wadded paper in the firebox, and found kindling to lay on top. He struck a match, trembling so with the cold that he could scarcely hold it steady. The paper blazed up and the flames began their little clinging dance around the splinters of pine. He laid on a few more sticks of wood, then closed the stove lid.

He pulled a chair up by the stove and set about removing his boots and socks. Now that he wasn't moving about, his body was beginning to itch as if he'd rolled naked in a patch of nettles. He began crying again.

"Big baby," he sobbed. "Got to stop this, got to get my boots off." His fingers were stiff and weak, and his bootlaces were frozen stiff. Finally, sobbing, he managed to work them loose. He clasped a foot in his hands, studying it. The skin was shriveled and wet, but with none of the white patches that would indicate frostbite. He remembered what Walter had told him. "Stay away from the heat. . . . Warm up as slow as you can."

Blubbering with self-pity, he took the dishpan down from the wall and stepped outside the cabin in his bare feet, not even bothering to look around first. He scooped snow into the pan and, returning to the cabin, set it on the stove to melt. "Water. Not hot water. Warm . . . that's what you use," he repeated over and over, like a dull schoolmaster.

He was thirsty. Terribly thirsty. The spring. He could get water there. He took the teakettle and went outside again, kneeling at the spring to drink a few sips of the dark clear water before filling the kettle. When he got back inside, he realized the cabin was slowly warming up. The snow in the dishpan had melted, and the water was beginning to steam.

At first the tepid water made his feet hurt even worse, tingling as if tiny animals were crawling all over them. After awhile, though, the water felt so good he decided to try it on his hands as well. For a few minutes, hunkered over, he forgot where he was. He sniffed his nose and realized he wasn't crying anymore, and his teeth had almost stopped chattering.

The kettle was steaming. He poured himself a cup of hot water and sipped it, feeling the warmth course its way through his body.

He added several chunks of wood to the fire. That was almost the last wood in the wood box, but it should last for a couple of hours or so, and he'd get more later, after he'd sat awhile. Right now, he just felt like sitting. The light from the stove flickered through cracks on the cast iron, casting little dancing patterns on the log walls. What light from outside that managed to find its way through the curtained windows was muted and gray. Maybe he should try to prop the door shut, so whoever was out there couldn't get in. Yes. That's what he should do. He tried to get up, then decided to wait for a minute or two. Right now he seemed awfully tired and comfortable. . . .

Seconds later he jerked himself upright and gazed frantically around the darkened room, trying to remember where he was. Olinger's. That was it. . . . He'd dozed off and nearly fallen off the chair. Mustn't doze off. Stay awake. Be ready. Wasn't anybody going to catch him sleeping!

He looked over at Olinger's cot. What if he just stretched out there for a few minutes? Olinger wouldn't mind. Olinger was off in Portland, or some place, on a toot. Wasn't that right? It all seemed so confused.

No. He'd better not lie down. Lying down would be a sign of weakness.

He needed a weapon. If he had to fight, he should have a weapon. There was Olinger's thirty-aught-six rifle, hanging on its pegs. But he didn't know where Olinger kept the shells, and besides, what if he hurt somebody?

In the dim light he saw perched on the table the chunk of pine that Olinger had been carving. A bird, wasn't it? It almost seemed to cock its head and look at him. Yes. A bird. If somebody came in, he'd throw the bird at him. He grabbed the little chunk. The wood felt comforting under his hand, and he began rubbing it, much as he used to rub the fur of his teddy bear when he was little. Nice birdy.

He was acting crazy, wasn't he? Maybe he'd better lie down for a few minutes. Get a little rest. Yes. He wouldn't close his eyes, though. That was a promise.

He rose to his feet, stiff-legged, and holding the bird in one hand, limped to the bed, snagging Olinger's old heavy overcoat from its hook and wrapping it around him. That ought to help keep him warm. Wish he had fresh socks—he'd look for those in a few minutes—after he'd rested. Olinger'd be sure to have fresh socks. Maybe he could fill a sock with a rock. Now, there'd be a real weapon. Sock with a rock . . .

He grabbed Olinger's pillow and plumped it up, then snuggled down in the cold bed, half sitting so he could keep a better eye on the door. He should prop a chair against the door. Yes. He'd do that. In a minute or two. He pulled the overcoat around him, feeling the rough scratch of coarse wool. He shifted his head against the pillow, smelling the warm, friendly Olinger odors. There. That was better. Holding tight to the little pine bird, he tucked the overcoat under his feet and arms, huddling down under the heavy fabric. Yes. Lots better.

The fire popped and crackled, sounding almost cheery. Something was bothering him. Something he'd noticed— no, something he hadn't noticed. What was it?

Drowsy with sleep, he wondered what they were doing at home. Jewel would be fixing supper and the radio would be playing and the lamps would be lit. He could almost smell the deep rich odors of food. . . . He wondered if they'd missed him by now. . . . He'd just rest for five minutes or so. Then he'd head for home. He'd be there in no time. Maybe he should prop the door shut. No. Didn't make sense. He'd be starting back down the mountain in a few minutes anyway. Didn't make sense to prop the door shut.

His eyes closed. He forced them open, but they closed again. The door was swaying in front of him, and there was Jewel, walking in with a steaming tray of food, smiling at him. He should thank her, but he couldn't make his mouth form the words. In a few minutes, he'd get up and have supper. Then he'd thank her. It wasn't good manners not to thank a person.

He clutched the little bird to his breast and snuggled deeper against the pillow. Nice little birdy—he'd show it to Olinger, the next time they all went up at the cabin to see him. There was something he wanted to ask Olinger too. Something he'd noticed the last time he'd seen him.

What a good pal Olinger was. But for now, he'd just hold on to the little birdy and sleep for another minute or two. Then he'd get up and have some supper. Then he'd go downstairs and play checkers with Shorty.

The fire popped and snapped again, settling down to a glowing bed of coals. But he didn't hear it. Hugging the pine bird, he smiled in his sleep.

10

Company

Sometime during the night, Harper stirred. Rough wool scratched against his cheek. It took a few seconds to remember where he was. Holding his breath, he lay on the lumpy cot, listening. Not a sound. Finally, he drew Olinger's overcoat to one side, limped to the window, and rubbed a bit of glass free of frost so he could peer out.

Snow was falling; big soft feathery flakes of snow, drifting down from the dark skies, filling the night with silence.

He stumbled back to the cot, his teeth chattering, and pulled the coat about him, trying to get warm. The fire was nearly out and the cabin was dark and cold. Against his will, he pictured the tiny clearing behind the shed; the jumble of pine boughs, the quilt, the gum boots, the snow falling on the old stubbled, defenseless, waxy face. He should put some kind of covering over Olinger, to protect him.

He tried to push the picture out of his mind. He didn't want to think about the clearing; didn't want to think about what he'd seen there. Olinger was dead; Olinger, with his licorice straps and generous laugh and clever gnarled hands. And there wasn't a thing he could do about it.

Besides, that wasn't Olinger out there. That was just his body.

He curled himself into a ball and pulled the coat tighter around him. He'd not think about Olinger. He'd go to sleep.

But he saw the clearing again, and the snow drifting down.

"I said I'm not going," he said aloud, defiantly. "He's dead. And whether I cover him or not, he's still dead."

But it didn't work. And there was something else too; something he'd missed when he found Olinger. What? Maybe, if he went back out to that dreadful place, he'd remember. And if he didn't go soon, it would be too late. The snow would do the job for him. And by spring, the body would be buried under ten feet of snow. No. He had to get some kind of shelter over Olinger. That was the first thing to do. Then he'd think what to do next.

Shivering with the cold, he threw the bed covering aside and pulled on his socks and wet boots. He threw the last few sticks of wood on the graying coals. A few minutes later, kerosene lantern in hand and a tarp and a length of rope slung over his shoulder, he closed the cabin door behind him, glanced warily about, and struck out in the direction of the shed. In the lantern light the snowflakes looked like goose down, falling straight toward him, as if he were their only target. The air was warmer than it had been, and smelled clean and fresh and scented with fir resin. Harper stuck out his tongue, and a flake landed on it, cold and elusive. For a second he forgot his terror and felt almost happy.

Only an inch or two of new snow had fallen thus far, and the hulking shadow of the shed loomed up sooner than he'd expected. Dreading the next few steps, he plodded around back. Snow was already mounding over Olinger's body.

He set down the tarp and rope and pried poles from the roof of the shed, stacking them upright, and tying their ends together like the frame of a tepee. He stretched the stiff canvas over the frame, wrapping it with rope to keep it in place, from time to time stealing a quick glance over his shoulder. But there was nothing to see; only somber trees and falling snow.

Hesitantly, holding the lantern, he crept inside the crude shelter, the yellowed light casting wavering shadows. He could smell the mysterious, tarry smell of warming canvas and the homely, friendly scent of burning kerosene. Hands shaking, he brushed the new snow from Olinger's face. The wound was dark, the color of a plum; a narrow scratch veered off from one corner, like a mistake on a drawing.

Gingerly, he poked at it with the blade of his pocketknife. Why, it was less than a quarter of an inch deep. He didn't know what a bullet hole would look like, but this sure wasn't one.

"That didn't do it," he muttered to himself. "Maybe somewhere else." He tugged at the quilt, smelling the odor of his own vomit, and feared for a moment he was going to be sick again. He squatted back on his haunches to steady himself. The walls of the tent waved in the lantern light, and the fumes were making his head spin. He needed fresh air. But he couldn't quit now. If he quit now, he'd never come back.

Moving the quilt, he examined Olinger's mackinaw. No cuts. And no blood. But what was this, clenched in Olinger's gnarled right hand? He moved the lantern closer. Flowers. A tiny bouquet of dried blue flowers.

Now, why would Olinger be holding flowers? He leaned forward and touched them with his mittened hand. They bent easily, then sprang back into place. Not dried flowers. Feathers. Blue feathers. He pulled one of them free, and saw the shiny black underlying color, and the bluish sheen, and the ivory quill. A blue jay.

A blue jay! That was the answer! Olinger had been carving a jay and needed some feathers to study. And he'd put on his mackinaw and his blanket and gone out to look for feathers, and had found some, and was carrying them along with him, planning to take them back inside, and he wasn't watching where he was going, and he'd hit his head on a tree stub—but it didn't hurt much, see, and then he came out here to look at the shed, and stepped into the hole, and . . .

Come on now. That didn't make sense. For starters, why was Olinger holding a handful of feathers? Did he put them there?

Or did someone else?

Don't think that!

What about his pockets? Maybe there'd be some clue in them.

He pulled the quilt down further, reaching first in one pocket, and then another. It was hard going; the body was heavy and awkward to move; the fabric stiff. He found a dime, and a small round greenish pebble, a piece of string, a stiffened handkerchief, a pocketknife, a bottle cap, a half plug of tobacco, cookie crumbs, a worn and folded scrap of tablet paper, another bottle cap, a tiny dried huckleberry. A black bead. A piece of white bark. A washer. An aluminum tax token. Lint.

But something was missing from this assortment. What?

His watch! That's what it was! Olinger's watch! Harper could see, as plainly as if it were happening right now, Olinger bringing out that watch and popping open the gold cover, showing him the beautiful white enameled face, with the finely wrought black hands, steady and antique as time itself. Where did he keep that watch? His shirt, wasn't it? Harper reached inside Olinger's mackinaw, feeling first one shirt pocket and then the other. One of the pockets still had the worn smoothness and bulge where the watch had been. But both were empty.

Maybe it had fallen when he wrapped the quilt around himself and lay down here.

Or was laid down by somebody. . . .

Don't think that!

Maybe he'd left it back at the cabin.

No, he wouldn't do that. Harper was remembering last summer. The last thing Olinger would do at night before climbing into bed was to wind up that watch and lay it on the little stand by his bed. "Like to hear it ticking away," he'd say. "Sounds friendly, during the night."

"Where'd you leave your watch, Olinger? Where's the watch?"

This was crazy; sitting and talking with a dead man in a makeshift tepee in the middle of the night. He had to get back to the cabin before he went completely wacky. And besides, the answers weren't here anyway. At least, he didn't think they were.

But there was something else; something he had to do, before he left.

He squatted there, remembering last summer and all the summers before: days when he'd chased pale ivory butterflies in the meadow and built dams in the tiny stream behind the house, hearing the peep peep of frogs; days of huckleberrying; days filled with the warm summer smells of pine and fir, the smells of mountain dust and fresh-cut kindling and wood smoke and potatoes frying; all those days, safe in the circle of Olinger's voice.

He had to say something. For Olinger. For those days.

A low wind moaned, stirring the canvas tarpaulin, and the lantern flame flickered. Harper hesitated, only half seeing Olinger's yellowed, sunken face. Then he began reciting the Twenty-third Psalm, haltingly, under his breath at first.

"The Lord is my shepherd, I shall not want. . . . He maketh me to lie down in green pastures. . . . He leadeth me beside the still waters. . . . He restoreth my soul. . . . He leadeth me in the paths of righteousness for His name's sake. . . . Yea, though I walk through the valley of the shadow of death, I shall fear no evil, for Thou art with me; Thy rod and Thy staff . . . they comfort me. . . . Thou preparest a table before me in the presence of mine enemies. . . ."

He had a lump in his throat and had to stop.

"Thou anointest my head with oil; my cup runneth over. . . . Surely goodness and mercy shall follow me all the days of my life; and I shall dwell in the house of the Lord forever. Amen."

He bent forward and kissed Olinger's cold, waxy forehead. He sat for a moment longer before pulling the quilt over Olinger's face. Lifting the lantern from where it had settled into the snow, he crept out of the improvised tent. Snow had already blanketed the canvas. Snow was falling thickly around him, obscuring the trees, making wheeling patterns in the air where the lantern swung its light, falling like a mantle on his head and shoulders.

Gosh, he was tired!

Something moved. Startled, he lifted the lantern and saw a dark figure, grinning wolfishly, emerge from the shadows.

11

Supper

Harper let out a yelp of terror. Then relief flooded through him. Moon! Snow dusted Moon's stocking cap, and the long pale scarf wrapped around his neck, and his heavy frayed mackinaw. His trousers from the knees down were hidden under stained canvas leggings, crusted with snow.

Stumbling through the darkness, Harper reached for Moon's hand, shaking his heavy mitten, trying to act grown-up. There was an instant—only an instant—when he felt a twinge of regret at being rescued. Now he'd never know if he could have managed by himself. For he *had* been managing by himself, hadn't he?

Moon struck a match with his thumbnail, the light illuminating his wolfish, crooked grin, and lit a cigarette. Harper grinned back, pushing out of his mind that traitorous thought. Oh, he was glad, yes, really glad, to see him. He gestured back toward the makeshift tent.

"Olinger—I found him. He's—dead. The snow—I thought maybe I should—you know . . ." He stopped. Whatever he was going to say didn't seem to be coming out right.

Moon nodded. He stamped his feet. Crusts of snow fell from the leggings.

Harper waited for him to say something, but Moon was silent. And now Harper could feel the questions beginning, and the doubts. How long had Moon been standing out here, anyway? Why hadn't he let him know he was here? Had he heard him praying, like some sanctimonious little twerp?

He hesitated, trying to think of the right words, the questions that would put everything back in its right place. Trying to sound easy, trying hard to look at Moon, he asked finally, "How'd you find me?"

"Tracks."

Of course! Harper felt a sudden wave of grateful acknowledgment. That made sense.

Another silence. Then, "You hungry?" Moon asked.

He couldn't have said a better thing. Suddenly Harper was hungrier than he'd ever been in his life. The questions could wait. "Starved."

They tramped back to the cabin; Moon, half hidden by the swirling snow, taking the lead. They built up the fire and filled the wood box. Harper set the kerosene lamp on the table and hung his coat on a chair to dry. He unlaced his boots and set them by the fire, not too close, then peeled off his socks, studying his blister. Moon was opening a big can of beans with the same heavy kitchen knife Harper had investigated so intently. He saw Harper looking at the blister. "Hurt?" he asked.

"A little."

Moon grunted. He finished opening the beans, dumped them in a pan, then stepped outside, returning in a few seconds with a tiny clump of moss, deep green in color. Tearing it into tiny shreds, he laid it in a rough weave across the blister. Then he got a roll of white adhesive tape from the store counter and wrapped Harper's foot. "Better?"

Harper nodded.

Moon rummaged in the chest at the foot of the bed, digging out a pair of wool socks, and another pair of thin cotton ones. He handed them to Harper; cotton first, then wool.

While Harper put on the dry socks, Moon spooned coffee from the can into the gray granite coffeepot and set it on the stove. He dipped a spoon in the beans and stirred them. A lovely, fragrant curl of steam filled the air. He took plates down from the shelf, and opened a box of soda crackers.

"Soup's on."

They ate in silence. Nothing in Harper's memory had ever tasted as good as those beans; the hot, sweet, mealy roundness of them, the pale brown syrupy juice, the slippery fatty bits of white pork. The coffee was perking, and the cabin was warm and aglow with lamplight; the air fragrant with the smells of wood smoke and beans and coffee. High up against the rafters, shadows of birds and bears, cougars and bobcats, swayed in and out of the darkness. He felt snug and safe and slow and sleepy. His feet were warm. The tape felt good on his blister. Any doubts he'd had about Moon were gone.

Moon sopped up the last bits of liquid on his plate and got to his feet. "More?"

Harper shook his head. "No thanks."

Moon got up from the table and started rummaging through the cans on the store shelf. "You like peaches?" he asked, opening a can and sliding the sections of fruit into two green glass bowls. He poured coffee into china mugs, then handed a tiny can of condensed milk to Harper. The smell of coffee reminded Harper of all those times the two of them had sat here at this same table with Olinger.

"I'll miss him," he said, sucking on a sweet slice of peach, feeling the comforting trickle of juice running down his throat.

Moon nodded. There was a long stretch of silence. Studying Moon's face in the lamplight, remembering last summer, remembering Olinger, Harper waited. Sometimes he had the feeling that before Moon used a word, he had to make it, much as he'd make something out of wood or stone or scraps of tin. But making things from wood or metal or string came easy to Moon; making words came hard. And it wasn't just putting words together that was hard; no, it was almost as if Moon had to invent new words every time he spoke.

"He . . . good . . . to me. . . ." The words trailed off.

Moon, his long fingers wrapped around his coffee cup,

stared into the distance as if he were watching something far away. He shook himself and took a swig of coffee. He leaned back in his chair and opened the stove door, settling the logs with the poker. The fire blazed and popped. The cabin glowed orange in the firelight. Harper finished his peaches, lifting the bowl to drink the last syrupy drops of juice. He felt reassured. Somehow, Moon had said enough.

"How'd you know I might try to come up here?"

Moon poured more coffee in his cup and offered the pot to Harper, who shook his head. "Come by the house— army give me a week before sending me to Fort Lewis. To say good-bye, they say." Moon laughed, a short, hard laugh. "How many people they think I say good-bye to?"

There was a short silence. "Well, you've got us."

Moon nodded. "Your momma say you at school. But then, when I go to the school, your teacher say you don't show up. That's when I think maybe you come up here."

"How'd you know Olinger was missing?"

Moon spooned more peaches into his own bowl. He shrugged. "News travel." He looked at Harper's empty bowl. "More?"

Harper shook his head.

"What about my dad? And Shorty?"

"Don't tell them. Go faster without them."

Harper slowly ate another slice of peach. Suddenly he was so tired he could hardly stay awake.

"Now what?"

"Sleep a couple hours, then start back."

The room was spinning around, and Harper kept trying

to hold his head up straight. He looked across at Moon, seeing two of him, then one, then two again. All he could think of was sleep. "Maybe we should wait a day or two," he muttered drowsily.

Moon shook his head. "Get snowed in. . . . You can't walk. . . . I put you on the sled."

"I can walk," Harper said, his voice thick. He managed one more sip of coffee. The next thing he knew, Moon was carrying him to the cot, his scratchy wool shirt rubbing against Harper's cheek. A sound—a lively, brisk, cheerful sound—alerted a memory, but before Harper could reflect on what the memory was, he was asleep again.

12

Heading Home

He woke once, or thought he woke. Moon's dark form was slouched in a chair by the fire, his arms wrapped around himself, his head buried deep in his chest. Drifting off, Harper half heard in the stillness the sound he'd heard earlier; the whiskery, businesslike oiled sound of tiny wheels and cogs, springs and gears, moving against one another in miniature perfection; over and over and over again.

Then Moon was standing over him, shaking his shoulder. The lamp was lit, and the worn plank floor gleamed. He could smell bacon frying and coffee boiling.

"Breakfast."

Harper's nose was stuffed up, and when he moved his whole body ached. "Is it still snowing?"

Moon nodded.

"What time is it?"

Moon shrugged. "Four . . . five."

Harper threw the heavy coat aside and tried to stand.

He was still fully dressed, except for his boots. His leg muscles were stiff, and his feet hurt. He hobbled to the table, holding on to the back of a chair to steady himself, and sat down. Moon poured a cup of coffee into a mug and set it on the table for him, along with a can of condensed milk and a spoon.

Harper poured the milk into the coffee and stirred it. He took a tentative sip.

"I guess I've made a fool of myself . . . sneaking off, coming up here, not telling anybody. Now I've got you in a mess too."

Moon seemed not to have heard him. He slid bacon onto a thick white plate and set it on the side of the stove to keep warm. He dropped biscuit batter in the hot bacon grease and watched as the globs of batter spattered and bubbled at the edges, turning them when the tops were brown. When they were done he dropped two of them onto each plate and added more batter to the skillet. He set one plate down for Harper and the other for himself. He took a half-empty jar of jam from the shelf and put it on the table, then sat down.

"Eat up," he said. "Help keep you warm."

Harper bit into a strip of bacon. It tasted wonderful. He smeared jam on a fried biscuit and ate it with his fingers, ignoring his fork. For a few minutes he thought of nothing but food, pushing away the thought of the journey that lay ahead.

"More?"

Harper nodded. Moon shoved more biscuits onto his plate, then stuffed the extras into an empty bread wrapper.

He carried his own empty plate to the sink, then reached up and lifted Olinger's sled down from the rafters. He wiped the dust from the wooden slats and waxed the runners with a block of paraffin. He looked around the cabin as if searching for something he knew should be there.

"Rope?"

Harper looked up from his plate. "I took it out to where I found Olinger."

Moon picked up a knife, threw on his coat and opened the door. Snow turned and tumbled like confetti. He disappeared into the gloom, shutting the door behind him.

Harper tentatively poked at his blister. It wasn't too bad. And his legs weren't as stiff now that he'd moved around, but his head was cottony with sleep. He pulled on his boots, dry and warm, and laced them up. He stacked the dishes in the sink. He should wash them, he knew. Olinger'd have a fit if anyone left dirty dishes in the sink.

Moon was back, stamping the snow from his feet. He laid Olinger's heavy coat in the sled, along with the biscuits, and a Hudson Bay blanket, and the jar with the remaining jam, and Olinger's steel-jacketed thermos. He tied the length of rope to the front of each runner. He banked the fire.

"Ready?"

Harper pulled his stocking cap down over his ears and put on his mittens. His heart was thumping in his chest. He nodded.

Moon blew out the lamp, and they left the cabin, pulling the door shut behind them. The sky was dark, with no hint of morning. Nearly a foot of snow had fallen during the night. Harper longed to run back inside where it was safe and warm.

But Moon was already moving out, dragging the sled. Harper stumbled along after him. In a few minutes he could feel his body adjusting to the cold. His eyes were watering and his nose ran, but his feet were warm enough; the two pairs of socks helped, and whatever the moss had been that Moon had put on his blister, it had drawn out the pain.

He settled down to the journey. One step at a time, he told himself. All he had to do was take one step at a time. Keep Moon's back in sight, keep moving. Every step was a step closer to home.

The image of Olinger kept running through his mind; Olinger . . . Olinger . . . Crazy to think that only yesterday he had imagined himself and Olinger making this trip back to the valley together. He winced at the thought. What a fool he'd been!

They passed the spot where the canyon fell off, down into the deep gorge of the Walla Walla River. The booming sound was silenced; all Harper could hear was the gravelly hiss of the wind and the sullen moaning of the firs.

He bumped against the sled. Moon had stopped and was looking at him.

Harper nodded. "I'm okay."

He could sense, rather than see, Moon nodding. Then they were off again.

How long they tramped on like that he could not say. At one point he fell. He managed to make it to his feet and staggered on. The snow was heavy; a weight against the front of his boots too heavy to push. Snow was in his eyes, his mouth. The whole world consisted of nothing but snow.

They were stopped. Moon was shoving a biscuit coated with jam down his throat. "Eat this," he said. Harper tried to swallow. Moon handed him a red plastic cup. "Coffee," he said.

Then they were off again. At one point he realized he was seeing the tops of trees, faint as ghosts in the snow. When he moved his head, he could still see Moon ahead of him, his back bent forward. He could hear the soft shushing sound of metal on snow. He felt a deep wave of shame. He must be on the sled, with Moon pulling him. He tried to sit up; to tell his legs to get moving. But nothing happened.

Now he was with Moon in a vast room, and it was cold. Moon had a bomb in his hand, and the bomb was ticking, louder and louder, and Moon was grinning at him, his wolfish grin. Olinger was there. Olinger had blue flowers in his hand. Blue feathers were spilling out of his mouth. He was laughing at Moon and pointing to the bomb. . . .

Harper opened his eyes. The sled had stopped. Moon was bending over him. He held a biscuit in his mittened hand. "Eat," he said. In the silence Harper thought he could hear the tick-ticking sound he'd heard back in the cabin.

Then he was asleep again.

He was in a huge tin barrel, and the barrel was rolling downhill, rattling and banging, and a man with a long fire hose was dashing him with cold water, covering his face with icicles. It was Moon, rubbing snow in his face.

"What! What's happening?"

Moon swept an arm in answer. Harper looked about, groggy with sleep. The snow was gone. A drizzle of rain was falling.

"You walk?" Moon was asking, his long face pale and drawn.

Harper threw Olinger's big coat aside and tried to stand. "Sure," he said. Promptly he fell down in the mud. He tried to rise, but couldn't.

Moon grinned at him; a tired grin. Then he wrapped Harper in Olinger's coat, tied a loop around his wrists and lifted him up. With Harper's body hoisted on Moon's back and Harper's arms wrapped around Moon's head, they started out again. Occasionally Moon slipped on the greasy mud, and once he nearly fell. But Harper knew none of this; all he was aware of was the warmth of Moon's back, and the cold drizzle of rain against his cheek.

He woke the last time to shouts. Through the drizzle he could see his father, wearing his old slicker, scrambling up the muddy road, gray-faced, in the rain to meet them, and Shorty, battered Stetson pulled down over his face, hobbling along behind. He could hear his father's voice.

"Son! Son!"

And Shorty's.

"You damn fool kid. . . . I ought to tan you good; 'ceptin' I'm so glad to see you!"

13

Homecoming

Danged if it makes sense to me," Shorty said. "Any of it."

It was late, but all of them, including Moon, were gathered around the supper table. The lamps were lit. A log shifted and groaned in the big living room heater.

"Let me see if I got this straight," Shorty said. "You said they was just one set of tracks—that would be Dave Titman and his hunting partner. Those tracks went to the cabin. But they wasn't any tracks out to where you found Olinger. Is that right?"

Harper nodded. He was surprised at the way Shorty was talking to him. Almost like he was a man. And here he'd expected to be treated like a child who'd done something wrong.

"Maybe they was there but you just didn't see them?"

Harper shook his head. He could scarcely keep his eyes open. "I don't think so."

"How about you, Moon? You notice any other tracks?"

Moon shook his head. He'd said little during the meal, as usual.

"And Olinger wrappin' hisself in a quilt like that. . . . It don't seem to me that's somethin' Olinger would'a did."

Harper felt the brief touch of Jewel's hand smoothing his hair. "We're tired, all of us," she said.

"Jewel's right," Walter broke in. "Harper's been over this story at least twice, Shorty. And you've asked some of these same questions fifteen times, seems to me. We can't expect to figure this whole business out tonight. I say we turn in."

He hesitated, then turned to Moon. "I guess I don't need to tell you how much we're beholden to you. Not many men I know could make the trip up that mountain and back on foot in less than twenty-four hours; not to mention carrying that big lug part of the way." He nodded toward Harper. "This crazy young buck here might have got himself killed if it hadn't been for you."

"Yes," Jewel added. "I—we'll—be grateful forever."

Moon flushed and looked down, fiddling with his spoon.

Walter looked at Jewel, as if silently asking her a question, then turned back to Moon. "I know you'll be leaving for the army in a day or two. But we'd be . . . honored . . . if you'd stay the night . . . stay as long as you can. We've got an extra bed upstairs. Or there's the bunkhouse, if you can put up with Shorty's snoring. It's probably warmer out there than it is upstairs."

Moon started to shake his head. Then he nodded. Yes. He'd stay in the bunkhouse.

Walter pushed his chair back. "Jewel, I'll just walk out there with these fellows; make sure that place isn't in such a mess that Shorty can't show it to company. Then I'm helping with the dishes. I'd appreciate your company if you can stay up a bit."

The men stood up, thanked Jewel for supper, and clattered out the back door. Harper kissed her, then felt his way up the stairs and down the hall to his room, too tired to pull the light string. A tree branch scratched against the roof overhead and a cold rain shush-shushed against the black windowpane. He opened the little trapdoor over the living room stove a crack to let in some heat, then undressed hurriedly, the linoleum floor cold and smooth beneath his bare feet. Maybe he'd wear his socks to bed, at least for a while, even though his mother disapproved.

When he had his pajamas on he pulled back the covers and crawled into bed, shivering, his teeth chattering. Burrowing down under the heavy quilts, he curled himself into a ball to keep warm.

Jewel's footsteps sounded on the stairs, and her silhouette appeared in the doorway, outlined against the faint light from downstairs.

"I thought you might be cold," she said. She lifted the cotton flannel sheets and tucked a towel-wrapped brick in by his feet. She patted the cover smooth. "There."

Harper stretched out, reaching for the cozy warmth. He was silent for a moment. "Mom?"

Jewel seated herself on the side of the bed. "Hmmm?"

"I'm sorry."

She bent down and laid her cheek against his. He could

smell the soft scent of dried roses and soap, and the smells of the kitchen. She sat up.

"Don't be."

"What?"

"Don't be sorry." She was silent for a moment. "That's not what I mean, either. Scaring us half to death. . . . you should be sorry."

Another silence. Then she sighed. "But you're growing up. I guess what you did was a part of that. . . ." She stroked his cheek with her hand. "In a way, I'm proud of you."

"It's Moon got me back. I'd never have made it."

"I know," Jewel said, "and I'm grateful to him. But you're the one who went up to Olinger's in the first place, when the rest of us were putting it off. And you'd have made it back by yourself, one way or another. You're tougher than you think. Like your father."

A delicious sense of warmth was spreading all around Harper, and he was so sleepy he could scarcely hear her voice.

"Harper?"

"Ummm."

"Just one thing. And then you can sleep. . . . About what you told us . . ."

Harper nodded.

"There are things you didn't tell, aren't there?"

He was so sleepy the words came out all mushed together. "Whadjamean?"

"Oh, just things. Things you forgot to say. Things you . . . maybe didn't want to say."

Suddenly Harper was wide awake, his heart pounding so loud in his chest he was sure Jewel could hear it. Thank God the room was dark, so she couldn't see his face! Everything he'd left out of his telling; the feathers pressed into the palm of Olinger's hand . . . his empty search for the watch . . . the quilt, not thrown over Olinger's shoulders like a shawl, but wrapped like a winding sheet . . . the feeling that someone had been following (leading?) him all day . . . the bird, falling through the sky . . . the ticking sound he'd waked to . . . (Had he imagined that?) . . . Why hadn't he told those things? He couldn't say, even to himself.

He gulped, knowing that what he was saying was a lie. "I told them everything I could remember. . . ."

Jewel stroked the blanket absentmindedly. "I know . . . I know. . . . And sometimes a person forgets things. . . . Sometimes things are just too . . . personal. Sometimes things don't make sense until you've thought them over."

Harper squirmed. What was she saying? What did she know? He'd never heard her talk like this before. It was almost as if she were someone else, not his mother. He tried to speak, to say something—anything—but Jewel placed her hand against his mouth. He could smell bread and onions and vinegar; the homey, safe smells of the kitchen.

"Don't," she said. "That's what I wanted to say. Just don't. You know more about that fine old man's last hours than anyone else on earth. But that doesn't mean you have to fritter away all you know by telling it to somebody else."

In the darkness her hand found a yarn tie on the blanket, and Harper could sense her fingers teasing at it. The wind was picking up, and rain slapped like a hand against the dormer window.

"I know you're tired, and I'll be finished in a minute. But I want to make sure you understand what I'm saying. You've been given a puzzle—a jigsaw puzzle. Or part of one. Pieces are still missing. And every time you tell your story, you lose another piece; the edges get blurred, and don't fit quite right, and before you know it, there's no way for you—or anybody else—to put the puzzle together." She paused. "Do you understand what I'm trying to say?"

Harper wasn't sure, but he nodded.

She was silent for a few seconds, then she spoke again, her voice urgent. "Say as little as you can. To me. To anyone. Until you've put the puzzle together. Otherwise, you may hurt someone."

What did she mean? Harper was afraid to ask.

"Promise?"

Yes, he promised.

Jewel laughed, a short, firm laugh. "Listen to me. I sound half spooky, like Tessie. . . . If I don't watch out I'll start studying the tarot, like she did."

She leaned over and kissed Harper on the forehead. Her lips were cool and distant. In the darkness he could just make out the strong beautiful curve of her cheekbone.

"Go to sleep now. You'll stay home from school for a day or two. I've already phoned Mrs. Emory."

* * *

Harper listened to her footsteps on the stairs. He heard the back door slam. He heard Walter's voice, then Jewel's. He heard the distant friendly clink of china and pots and pans in the kitchen, and the rush of water being drawn from the faucet. The rain beat at his window again, fierce and spiteful. But the brick at the foot of his bed was warm. He'd go to sleep now. He straightened out. He had the idea that if he lay straight at night he'd grow tall. Maybe six feet. That's why he always slept straight as an arrow, all night long.

He lay waiting for sleep.

But sleep wouldn't come.

What was the matter? Here he was, safe at home. Even Shorty seemed halfway proud of him.

Why then did he feel so melancholy? Well, in the first place, now that he was in his own bed, safe, he had time to think about what had really happened. Olinger was dead. That was going to hurt for a long time, knowing he'd never see Olinger again, never again hear his wheezy laugh, never again feel his gnarled old hand across a shoulder. It was like he was saying good-bye to Olinger. But that wasn't all of it. No. He was telling something else good-bye, as well, but he didn't know who or what he was saying that good-bye to.

What was it Jewel had said? "It's your puzzle. Don't give it away." She'd never talked to him like that before. But that shouldn't make him feel so sad, should it? He should feel happy. Wasn't he growing up?

Well, he'd think about it tomorrow.

The rain pelted against the window again, and the tree branch scratched against the roof overhead. But Harper didn't hear them this time, for he'd just remembered something. . . .

He was five, and it was a summer afternoon, late. He was playing by himself out by the tiny brook, scarcely the width of a man's hand, that meandered past Olinger's store. He was trying to catch a frog, green as a lima bean and no larger than one, so quick it dodged his every effort. He gave up finally and started building a dam, pressing rocks into place and chinking them with shreds of the gray tree moss—the kind that always reminded him of an old man's beard. Already the water was backing up, smooth as a china plate.

Out of the corner of his eye he could see the men in their dusty Levis and sweat-stained shirts sitting outside the cabin, visiting. Olinger whittling, as usual, his black elastic storekeeper armbands describing a slow dance as he carved away at a piece of pine. He had a cigar in his mouth, and now and then Harper caught a rich whiff of cigar smoke.

". . . Paddie was . . ." he heard his father begin to say. Harper looked up, trying to catch what he was saying, but all he could hear was the rich burr of his father's voice. Shorty laughed once, that soft, knowing chuckle of his, in the middle of Walter's story.

But look at Olinger! He'd stopped his whittling. He took the cigar from his mouth and sat unmoving until Walter was finished. A long, long silence hung in the air. Then Olinger said one word: "Paddie!"

Harper remembered now the way that word had sounded; hard and flat as a piece of shale. And Olinger's mouth; as though he'd bitten into a quince.

The old man turned his head and spat. The silence continued. His father cleared his throat. Shorty took off his Stetson and fanned himself. A minute later Walter stood up, dusted himself off, and called for Harper.

There were the usual good-byes. Olinger brought a long black licorice from the store and gave it to Harper. "One for the road," he said, the same as always. He handed Walter a pint jar of huckleberries and a handful of mountain flowers; Indian paintbrush, jack-in-the-pulpit, woodbine, wild roses. ". . . For Jewel."

But Harper could feel the stillness inside his father and Shorty, like boys who'd just received a reprimand from their favorite teacher. . . .

There was a sudden gust of wind, and another burst of rain.

Why should he think of that afternoon now? He sighed once and snuggled down farther in the covers, feeling for the warm brick, curling up in a tight ball. Tomorrow night he'd lie straight. For sure.

The rain struck the double-hung window again; a burst so hard that a few drops found their way in between the panes and trickled down over the faded wallpaper.

But Harper didn't hear.

14

Sheriff

Watery midmorning sunlight streamed in the window. Harper lay for a moment, listening to voices floating up from downstairs. One of them was Walter's. The other he didn't recognize. Throwing the heavy covers aside, he reached for his clothes, his body stiff and aching. His boots proved impossible. Finally he hobbled down the cold stairs in his stocking feet, carrying his boots in his hand.

The kitchen windows were steamed over, and the room smelled of apples and cinnamon and steam. Jewel was standing over a large vat, placing glass jars in the water. Walter sat at the kitchen table, peeling and coring apples, a box of apples on the floor beside him. Across from Walter, in uniform, sat a large man with a coarse-skinned face and red hair. A campaign hat sat squarely on the table in front of him, and a cup of coffee steamed at his elbow.

"Well, look who's here," Walter greeted Harper. "I was just ready to come up and wake you." He fitted another

111

apple into the peeler. "Son, this is Sheriff Gooler from Umatilla County. He drove over from Pendleton this morning to talk to you, after I reported Olinger's death."

The sheriff stood up and reached for Harper's hand. "Glad to meet you, son," he said. His voice was rich and mellow, a politician's voice. His leather puttees were burnished with age, and his wool gabardine shirt was pressed in straight lines down the front, pulling tightly across his belly. His Sam Browne belt was slung low, weighted down by his beautifully polished Colt .45 revolver.

"I saved some breakfast for you," Jewel said, glancing at Harper. "But wash up, first—Walter, I'm going to start filling jars now. Maybe you could give me a hand with the lids. They're in that pan there."

The sheriff sat down again and reached for his coffee cup. "You do what your mother says, and then I'd like to have a little man-to-man talk, if you don't mind. You know, little lady," he said across the room to Jewel, "there's nothing quite like canning time. And there's nothing smells as good as apple pie."

Jewel set a plate with toast and scrambled eggs at the table just as Harper returned from the bathroom, wet hair slicked back. "More coffee?" she asked the sheriff.

The sheriff beamed at her. "Thank you, pretty lady." He looked at Harper. "So you're the brave young man that found that old fellow dead up in the mountains."

Harper had his mouth full of egg and toast. He tried to nod. The sheriff sipped his coffee. "Now, son, what was your name again? I don't believe I caught it." Harper told him.

"I see. And, Harper, you must be about, what, four-teen—fifteen?"

He shook his head. "Twelve."

"No! Why, I'd have thought, just seeing you there, you must be at least a sophomore in high school. You've got that look about you, Harper. Grown-up. You know what I mean?"

Harper shook his head again. He blushed.

"Well, you could have fooled me." Sheriff Gooler pulled a pad from his shirt pocket and felt in his trousers for a stub of pencil. "Now, Harper, what I'd like to do is to have you just relax and tell me all you can remember. Everything. Even if it don't seem important to you. And then, when you're finished, I'll ask you a few questions. Okay?"

Harper nodded. The sheriff spoke to Jewel, who had returned to her canning. "Say, little lady, this is great coffee. You got any cream and sugar, by chance?"

Jewel brought a cream pitcher and a jar of honey to the table. "No sugar," she said. "Rationed."

Harper couldn't help but notice the coolness in her voice. But the sheriff just laughed. "Come on, come on. You farmers got all the sugar you want. Everybody knows that."

"Go ahead, son," Walter said from the kitchen counter, where he was screwing lids on jars full of apple slices. "Tell the sheriff what you know."

For just a moment, Harper remembered vaguely what Jewel had said to him last night. On the other hand, if he didn't tell what had happened, he'd be breaking the law, wouldn't he? And the sheriff seemed so—well, important. Hesitantly, Harper started in, trying to tell everything in order, leaving out all the embarrassing things, like, say, throwing up all over Olinger's mackinaw.

The sheriff stirred cream and honey in his coffee while he listened. He took a long sip, and another. A tiny drop of coffee dripped onto his shirt front and he wiped it off with his red hand, trying not to show his annoyance. From time to time he nodded, full of sympathetic understanding. When Harper was done, the sheriff sat for a moment, silent. Hmmm! his expression seemed to say, maybe this wasn't quite as open and shut as he'd thought.

"That's it?"

Harper nodded. He felt disappointed. He hadn't exactly expected—well, applause—but still . . . hadn't he done all right?

The sheriff belched softly. "Excuse my French—Now, Harper, look here. We've got a serious matter on our hands. There's a dead man laying up there, and all you can tell me is that you played hookey from school and rode halfway up that mountain on your bike and found Orender or whatever his name was out behind his cabin dead and then you came back down with this Moon fellow who just happened to stop by. Now, I'm the expert, but I need your help to see that justice gets done. I can tell, just by looking, you're bright. Why, I'll bet if you tried you could fill a book with what you remember. But what you know won't do us a nickel's worth of good unless you tell me. So what I'm going to do, Harper, is ask you a few simple questions, sort of prompt your memory. That fair?"

Harper nodded, determined to be as helpful as he could. And he liked the sheriff—sort of—the way he seemed so interested and friendly and all. Although he didn't think the sheriff should call his mother "little lady." That seemed—well—forward. Cheap and forward; that's what she'd probably call it. On the other hand, if anybody could figure out this puzzle—because that's what Jewel had said it was, wasn't it, a puzzle?—then for sure the sheriff was that person.

"Good boy. Now let's get started. Now tell me, Harper, what was—er—Olinger wearing when you found him?"

He answered the sheriff's first question, and as soon as he'd finished, the sheriff was ready with another one. He asked in what direction the body lay. Did Harper think it was a grave or a sunken place in the snow? How was the quilt wrapped? Could Olinger have done that himself? What footprints did he find? Any peculiar smells? How well did the family know Dave Titman? What did the cabin look like inside? How well did he know this fellow Moon? . . .

Oh, there were some things the sheriff didn't ask him about and Harper didn't volunteer: the watch, and finding those feathers in Olinger's hand, and hearing those miniature brisk, businesslike sounds in the night. No use bothering him with all that. Or telling him about last summer, and Buck and Jeeter. Even Olinger had said that wasn't anybody's business but theirs.

He was telling about how Moon happened to come up looking for him. The sheriff had said this would be the last question. Jewel was standing at the stove, intently stirring sugar syrup for the apples. Her back was straight and fine. For an instant, catching sight of her like that, he almost forgot what he was saying.

"And where's Moon now?"

Walter spoke up from the kitchen. "He's gone."

"Isn't he . . . ," Harper started to say, but Walter interrupted.

"He spent the night here, but he left early this morning, before any of us were up."

"You mean Moon's gone?" Harper turned to his father. "Without even saying good-bye?"

Walter left the kitchen and pulled up a chair at the table. He cleared his throat. "Sheriff, I think maybe Harper's told you as much as he knows."

Sheriff Gooler pulled himself up straight and looked across the table at Walter. Looking at the two men, Harper thought how undistinguished his father appeared, by comparison.

"Now, Walter," the sheriff said, "I just met you this morning, but I can tell by looking at you that you're not the sort to obstruct justice. I've a few more questions to put to this fine lad here, Walter, and then I'm going to need to speak to this Moon character. He sounds like the kind of riffraff, if you'll excuse my saying so, that it pays to keep an eye on."

"Riffraff!" Harper couldn't believe what he was hearing. Calling Moon riffraff! Who did that sheriff think he was!

Walter's bald head glistened. "I don't believe you understood me, Sheriff. I said no more questions. That's final.

And now about Moon. I don't know where he is, but I can tell you this: He risked his neck to save my son's life. Anybody does that's not riffraff in my book. And I know this too; he joined the army last week, scarcely eighteen, when it would have been easy enough for him to get deferred, like I see a lot of folks doing. If I were you, I believe I'd just treat this matter for what it is; an old man— a fine man, one of the best I ever had the honor of knowing—dying all alone up in the mountains."

The sheriff rose stiffly from his chair. His face was flushed. "Well, Walter, I'm always sorry when somebody like you, decent and well-meaning, gets in the way of justice. But I don't hold a grudge, Walter. No sirree. I'll be talking to this here Moon fellow, one way or another. You can bet on that. And I'll bet something else too. You'll be glad I did."

He picked up his campaign hat, holding it carefully by the brim so as not to smudge the felt. "You'll be hearing from me," he said. He turned and nodded toward the kitchen. "Thank you for the coffee, little lady. And good luck with your apples."

15

Winter Gifts

For a few minutes after the sheriff, starch-backed, left the house, Harper was afraid to look in Jewel's direction. He had, suddenly, the feeling he'd talked too much. But then, in the middle of ladling syrup into jars, she began whistling "Bye Bye Blackbird." Walter, standing next to her, put his arm around her. "How about a kiss, little lady?" he asked. She turned and threw her arms around him. "Oh, Walter!" she said, laughing, "I do love you!"

"That big bag of wind!" Walter said. "Who does he think he is! Playing detective with my son and making eyes at my wife at the same time!"

"But is it true?" Harper interrupted. "Is Moon really gone? Without even saying good-bye?"

Walter nodded. Shorty had waked sometime during the night, it seemed, and found Moon's cot empty. Walter said he wasn't surprised. Moon was supposed to catch a train to Fort Lewis today to be inducted. And besides, a bunkhouse might seem too close to civilization for some-body like him.

"What about the sheriff?" Harper asked. "Won't he try to stop him?"

Walter shook his head. He laughed. "Somehow, I doubt the U.S. Army's going to pay that tinhorn sheriff much attention. Unless something peculiar turns up. Now Jewel, if you don't need me around anymore, I believe I'll go on up to the barn and help Shorty mend sacks."

Something "peculiar," to use his father's word, did turn up a few minutes later. At Jewel's urging, Harper had gone upstairs to fetch his schoolbooks. "After you get some homework done you can take a nap on the daven-port, where it's warm."

His room was icy cold, but he took a minute to straighten his bed, tugging the heavy quilts back in place. When he lifted the pillow he saw a tiny package, wrapped in brown paper and tied with a bit of sack twine. In one corner he could make out a faint penciled drawing of a harp, the kind he imagined Irish poets fancying. How long had it been there? Certainly, he hadn't felt it under his pillow last night, or heard its rustle. But then, the paper was crumpled and worn, and the package so soft and light he could very well have lain on it and never known its presence.

Shivering with the cold, he unwrapped the twine. The dark, wild, tangled mushroom smell of the mountains came to him. Moss. The same dried moss Moon had used on his blister. Did that really happen, any of it, night before last? It seemed like a hundred years ago. There was something else too hidden beneath the moss. A tiny blue feather, with every barb smoothly in place. Gingerly, Harper held it up, turning it over and over, searching for clues that couldn't possibly be there. Jewel's whistling floated up from the kitchen: "Bye Bye Blackbird."

What did it mean? Had Moon put it there last night, while he slept? How could he have done that? And if so, why? A going-away present? A sign? There was no way to know. But there was one thing he did know. He *hated* that sheriff, daring to think that Moon had anything to do with Olinger's death! Replacing the feather in its bed of moss, he stuffed it back under his pillow and hurried downstairs, back to the warm kitchen stove and the dull pleasure of schoolwork.

The long, slow day passed. He did two pages of arithmetic and diagrammed eight sentences. He drew a map of Chile. He studied South American rubber plantations in his geography book, falling asleep after the first page. He ate homemade doughnuts snatched from the bubbling pot and dusted with powdered sugar and cinnamon. After supper he played checkers with Shorty and lost; twice.

That night, lying in bed, a flannel-wrapped brick at his feet, warm at last, he pulled the little tattered bundle from under his pillow, smelling the dark, rich earthy smells of moss and the imagined perfume of birds in sunlight.

Clutching the fragile bundle of earth and sky next to his cheek, Harper realized—no, half realized—something important. He'd made a choice when he'd climbed on his bike and started up the mountain, looking for Olinger.

His own choice; nobody else's. All those crazy things that had happened—Olinger dead, wrapped in his own quilt; Moon appearing out of nowhere in the middle of a snow-filled night; that bird, dropping like a collapsed umbrella through the dying late afternoon sky—they weren't part of some spooky mumbo jumbo, like Shorty was fond of talking about. They were parts of that journey; pieces of the real world; sad, happy, frightening, strange, mysterious—but real. Always real.

Like this package, fragrant next to his cheek. He didn't know how it got there. Or what, if anything, it meant. But, if he chose to, he could try to find out. If he chose to. That was the important part. The choice was up to him. That half-realized fragment of thought drifting around in his head, he fell asleep.

That nighttime insight, shiny as hope when it first appeared, faded over the next few weeks. Life returned to normal. School. Chores. Homework. Piano lessons. The weather was dreary. Day after day, low clouds hung over the valley. Earth and sky merged into a soft, dim woolly gray. A stillness settled over the countryside, and even the rangy growl of the bombers flying practice missions out of the army air base was subdued and peaceful.

The *Walla Walla Union Bulletin* ran a four-line story about Olinger: LONGTIME MOUNTAIN MAN FOUND DEAD. Unfortunately, they spelled Harper's name wrong; "—The body was discovered by Happer McDowell"—and that took away considerably from the pleasure of seeing his name in print.

The army turned down Sheriff Gooler's request for extradition. Shorty heard that news one afternoon while he was at Brinker's Hardware, buying nails. "That'll put that swell-headed sheriff in his place," Walter said upon hearing the news. Harper agreed.

But except for the sheriff, no one seemed very interested in Olinger's death. The faraway war was on everyone's mind. In Africa, Rommel and his panzer troops were being driven back to the Mediterranean, strewing mine fields behind them in hopes of slowing down the British. War correspondents described battles fought under brilliant desert skies. Sitting by the stove and reading the newspaper during the gloomy days of winter, Harper could scarcely begin to imagine Egypt, with its hot desert sands and glittering palms.

General MacArthur had moved his headquarters to the island of New Guinea, and American and Australian troops were fighting the Japanese in the jungles of the South Pacific.

Captain Eddie Rickenbacker, whose plane had disappeared in late October, was rescued, along with six of his crew, from a raft six hundred miles north of Samoa. "God heard our prayers and answered them," Rickenbacker said in an interview.

Harper read the story and studied the pictures of Rickenbacker and his men. They were skinny and burned from the fierce southern sun, but they grinned and waved like kids at the camera. Harper laid down the paper and stared out the window at the bleak wintry foothills of the Blue Mountains. What was Moon doing? he wondered.

Was he still at Fort Lewis? Maybe, by now, he was halfway across the world in some far-off place: Europe, the South Pacific, Georgia.

If Moon were here, maybe the two of them would head back up to Olinger's to take a look around. But that would be impossible, even for Moon. There was at least ten feet of snow up there by now, and besides, even if they could get there, what would they look for? There was, granted, still the puzzle of Olinger's watch. And Harper couldn't get over that half-dream he'd had at the cabin, the ticking sound, and Moon, asleep in a chair. But shoot! You could buy a good pocket watch, an Ingersoll, for a dollar. Suppose he *had* heard a watch that night. That didn't mean it was Olinger's. Why, that would be stealing! And Moon wouldn't steal.

He took to roaming the neighborhood every day after school, in the brief hour before darkness, poking through abandoned barns and sheds. Where had Moon lived? If he could find that place, maybe he'd find clues there; letters, something Olinger might have given him, something he could show the sheriff, to prove once and for all that Moon was innocent.

In one cold, dark barn set back in a grove of cottonwoods, down by the river, he almost stumbled over two third graders from school playing doctor. They hid under a dingy blanket when he stepped into the manger where they'd set up office. Harper left, pretending he hadn't recognized them. Outside another shed, next to the railroad tracks, a hobo, his hands and face sooty as a chimney sweep's, was cooking beans in a coffee can over a small fire. Harper could see his bedroll, with an apple box serving as a table, in the dim shadows. He greeted Harper with a toothless grin and offered him a bowlful of beans. Harper declined, with thanks.

After he'd arrived home late five days in a row, Jewel asked him what he was up to. Harper said he'd been helping Mrs. Emory, but that he was finished now. After that he started coming home earlier. Anyway, he'd just about run out of places to explore. There was No-Man's-Land, an abandoned farm down by the river, but the place gave him the willies, and he thought he'd put off going there until, maybe, spring.

The Christmas season drew near, and Moon sent them a card. Studying it on the way in from the mailbox, Harper experienced a great warm feeling of relief. There wasn't any message; just the family name and address in block print, and a tiny crescent-shaped drawing. But at least Moon was safe. Later, upstairs in his room, he tried to compare the writing with the picture of the harp. He realized that this was the first time he'd ever seen anything Moon had written.

He planned Christmas gifts, making, with Walter's help, a small cedar chest for Jewel. He braided Chinese pheasant tail feathers into a hatband for Shorty's old Stetson. What to get Walter puzzled him until one Saturday in town he saw a beautiful blue satin tie with a picture of a rainbow trout leaping for a fly painted on it. In the distance could be seen the tiny figure of a fisherman, net in one hand and fly rod in the other. He asked how much it was. The clerk told him it was genuine hand-painted and a bargain at $1.25.

Harper didn't have that kind of money. But working alone at night out in the bunkhouse, he managed to reproduce the scene on one of Walter's old ties. True, when he finished the tie was stiff as a board, and smelled of turpentine. But Christmas morning, when the presents were opened, Walter seemed pleased.

On New Year's Eve, the family stayed up late. Jewel wore her dark blue wool dress with a cream-colored lace shawl over her shoulders, and Walter had on his tie. Even Shorty dressed up for the occasion, wearing a frayed white shirt he'd ironed himself—you could see the scorch marks—and a red bandana tied around his wrinkled neck.

They ate supper by candlelight, and later carried the candles into the living room, where they listened to radio reports of New Year celebrations. Times Square in New York City was dimmed, and the tooting of horns and the ringing of church bells sounded muffled. America was in the middle of a war, the solemn-voiced commentator reminded them, but there was hope. Only a few days earlier, American bombers, in one of their biggest raids yet, had flown over Germany, dropping hundreds of two-ton block-busters on Munich. The Russian army, well into its winter campaign, was advancing at the rate of thirty miles a day, hoping to capture the eastern German army, estimated at a million men, in the Caucasus. A Japanese naval force had been rebuffed by American bombers at Guadalcanal, and MacArthur announced that the Japanese fortifications near Buna had been taken with great loss of life for the enemy.

"I'd sure like to know what Moon's up to," Walter said after they'd turned off the radio. "I wouldn't be surprised but what he might be in the thick of things by now."

Jewel shook her head. "I hope not." A candle flickered, then grew steady again. "Wind's picking up," Shorty said, cocking an ear.

Jewel got up from her chair. "I made mulled cider," she said, forcing a bright tone, "to toast the New Year. Harper, maybe you'd like to help me bring it in." When they returned to the living room, Harper passed around the steaming mugs.

"Here's to peace," Walter said, raising his mug.

Tentatively, they sipped at the hot cider. It was good: spicy, hot, and too sweet—just the way Harper liked it.

"And to all those we love and have loved, wherever they are," Jewel added, her face beautiful in the dim candlelight.

"I'll drink to that," Shorty said, uncustomarily ceremonious and solemn.

Harper drank the rest of his cider, along with the others, but the toast left him feeling melancholy again. He felt he was marking time, waiting for something—he didn't know what—to happen.

16

Tractor Ride

In late February a few mild days set in, and Walter taught Harper to drive the homemade tractor. Sitting up high on the steel seat, enveloped in the warmth of the engine heat, playing the gas pedal like a musical instrument while the men loaded cuttings and dead branches onto a low wagon, he thought he'd found his place in life.

One sunny afternoon in April, home from school and putting off piano practice, he wandered out toward the orchard, looking for something to do. He'd just about made up his mind that this was the day to hike down to the river and explore No-Man's-Land—his detective work had slowed to a stop—when the tractor, sitting idle next to the packing shed, caught his eye.

He had strict orders not to fool around with the tractor when the men weren't there. But today seemed like an exception. He'd go to No-Man's-Land on Saturday, he decided, when he had more time.

He started the motor, put the tractor in gear, and drove

around to the front of the shed. Here the pasture sloped gently down to the creek. The new grass was green and slick, and he could feel the wheels slide beneath him when he cornered. He pressed a little harder on the gas pedal. This was fun!

The wind lifted his cap from his head. He pulled to a stop, jumped off the tractor, leaving the engine idling, and ran to fetch it.

He had the cap in his hand and was on his way back to the tractor when he saw that it had begun to move; creeping down the little slope toward the creek, very slowly, but picking up speed.

He started after it, knees high, cap in hand. What if it rolled into the creek? No way could he hide that. He could see it, sitting like a mechanical water buffalo in the middle of the stream. He could imagine too what Walter and Shorty would say: "Told you never to drive that tractor when we weren't around!" And he'd never forgive himself, either, for being so dumb.

He skidded once and nearly fell. But the tractor wasn't moving all that fast, and in a few seconds he was alongside, the warm exhaust heady as perfume. He grabbed for the seat brace to hoist himself up, gulping with relief. He'd averted a major disaster.

Maybe his foot hit a gopher hole. Maybe it was just the wet grass. But his ankle gave way beneath him. The metal brace slipped from his fingers, and he was falling.

The sky was whirling above him, and the roar of the engine was in his ears. He struggled to regain his balance, but he couldn't. He felt the sharp hot metal of the manifold next to his face, and smelled the sweet damp smells of earth and freshly crushed grass.

He tried to roll to one side, but a wet heavy rear tire was climbing up on his belly, pressing harder and harder, until all he could see was black. And then he fainted.

He must have come to almost immediately. At first, lying there, perfectly still, he was amazed at how peaceful he felt. The April sky was all airy and blue, and the color was deep and rich, with an occasional luminous cloud, fat as an unshorn sheep, floating past. He waited for the pain to start, but after a few minutes, decided that maybe he'd been lucky. There wasn't going to be any.

Lazily, he wondered what had happened to the tractor. He tried to raise his head for a look, but decided not to; it seemed like too much work. Besides, he could hear it idling quietly, some distance away. It must have stopped before it reached the creek.

He thought again about getting up, and was just on the verge of doing so, when he felt a dribble of moisture oozing from his mouth. He reached a finger up and daubed around, then looked at his finger to see if it was red. No, he wasn't bleeding. He tried wiggling his toes, lifting himself slightly to get a look at them. They moved just fine. The movement made his stomach hurt, though, so he lay back down again. He'd rest for a while.

He wondered if he could see where the tractor tire had rolled over him. Gingerly he loosened his trousers and pulled up his shirt, peering down at his belly. Not a mark. He pressed the skin to make sure he wasn't imagining things. Amazing! It had rolled over him, hadn't it?

He tried to button his trousers, but it seemed like too much trouble. "I'll wait a few minutes," he said to himself. It was very comforting to hear his voice, and he decided to talk to himself again, but couldn't think of anything to say.

Just then, though, a robin fluttered to the ground a few feet away and watched him for what seemed like a very long time. "Hello, robin," he said.

Now wasn't that nice, having company? The robin just stood there on its skinny little bird legs, and said nothing. It looked reasonably friendly, though. "I'll bet you think I'm some new variety of worm," Harper said, trying to make conversation. The robin continued to stare at him. Then it cocked its head and hopped away. He was sorry to see it go. It had seemed like a nice bird. Maybe his conversation had bored it.

The moisture from the grass was beginning to seep through his clothes, and he noticed that he was beginning to feel a little chilly. "I guess I'll get up," he said aloud, in a matter-of-fact voice.

He felt a mild pang of disappointment, realizing he wasn't hurt. He'd had a brief vision of himself with a plaster cast encasing one leg, hobbling gamely about on crutches. Wouldn't that be something!

On the other hand, summer was less than two months away, and who wants to wear a cast in the summer?

"I'm not hurt," he said aloud, as if the robin were still

there. "I'll get up now. But I don't think I'll drive the tractor anymore this afternoon."

He rolled over to one side and raised his head from the matted grass. His insides felt like scrambled eggs, but that probably didn't mean anything.

He drew his legs back to give himself leverage, and pushing at the ground, lifted himself to his knees. He rested there for a moment, staring at the cottonwood trees marking the course of the Walla Walla River down by No-Man's-Land, half a mile away. The ends of their branches were just beginning to turn the palest green, and the trunks were a tawny color. He hadn't noticed that before.

Something was wrong, though. The trees seemed to be moving, and the light on them was uncertain; now bright and clear, now filled with darkness. He looked at them again, trying to hold them fast, trying to stop their dancing.

The darkness was coming faster now, great rays of it flashing down from the sky, shattering like glass all around him. Then the darkness was inside his head, and all he could see was darkness.

With a soft thud, his body hit the ground.

The next thing he remembered was voices, a long way off, and curtains of light, dense as summer fog. He tried to push at the curtains, to move them away so he could see better, but nothing happened.

Slowly the mist drifted away, and there was Walter, his face ruddy and drawn with concern; and Shorty, wet straggles of hair plastered to his skull, fanning him with his stained cowboy hat. The braid of pheasant feathers had already begun to fray and lose their sheen. He'd have to fix those.

"There now," Walter was saying. "There now, son. Just take it easy. Don't try to move."

"Dammit, boy . . . ," Shorty broke in. "You and your goldanged tricks! You gave us one helluva scare! You're not too old to get the seat of your trousers warmed. And if your daddy won't do it, I just may have to. You hear me?"

Harper tried to nod.

Walter turned to Shorty. "Stay here and don't let him move. I'll get the truck."

Half an hour later Harper was lying on the examination table at Saint Mary's Hospital with Walter and Jewel standing on one side, and the doctor, his white-smocked belly as expansive as a snowfield, on the other. The doctor pressed on Harper's groin and belly with heavy fingers. "That hurt? That?" Moving his hand from one spot to another, he repeated the question.

Harper tried to decide when to nod yes and when to nod no. He couldn't tell any difference from one spot to the other; it all hurt. "The boy's fractured his pelvis, but that's about the size of it," the doctor announced finally.

"What are you going to do?" Walter asked.

"Get him in a cast to keep him from moving around too much. Tomorrow, we'll send him home. Jewel, you keep him in bed and don't let him move. Don't even let him sit up, for the first week or two. He'll be all right, if he's careful."

"How long?"

"In bed, you mean? A month, at least. More, if he gets rambunctious and won't lie still."

The doctor's florid face hovered over him. "You hear that, son?" he asked. Harper nodded. A month! When spring was here. It might as well be forever.

"And don't go feeling sorry for yourself!" the doctor added. "It's a wonder to me that tractor didn't make mincemeat of your whole insides. You got lucky!"

And so, through the remainder of April and into May, while the other eighth graders were putting in their last weeks at Springdale School, playing softball, riding bikes, planning picnics down at Whitman Monument, testing the river to see if it was warm enough to swim in, Harper lay in a bed Walter had set up for him in the living room, watching the locust trees blossom with ivory-colored flowers, smelling their faint perfume, counting the days until he was free again.

No-Man's-Land—everything—would have to wait.

17

Soldier's Medal

It was a late afternoon in the first week of May. It had showered earlier in the day, but the rain had moved east, hiding the Blue Mountains, turning the snow to slush. Harper was sitting up in bed—the bed where he'd spent the last three weeks—working on a model of a P-41 fighter plane, when he saw someone turn in at the far end of the lane, picking his way around the mud puddles, heading for the house.

He shoved the blueprints and sheets of balsa wood aside. Moon! It was Moon, dressed in his army uniform, the brass buttons glinting dully on the long woolen jacket. Even in a uniform, though, Moon didn't look like a soldier. It wasn't just the way his clothes fit, it was that loping, independent walk of his, catlike, half wild. No soldier walked like that.

"Mom!" he called to Jewel, out in the kitchen, whistling a tune while she got supper ready. "Look who's coming in the lane!"

The whistling stopped. "Who?"

"Moon. And he's wearing his uniform."

Moon made his way down the slope past the barn and up the path under the silver maples toward the house. He caught sight of Harper peering through the window, and gave him an awkward, half-military salute, and his old familiar sardonic grin. A wide-brimmed cap was pulled low over his narrow forehead, but his face looked the same. No, not quite. Something was changed, although at first Harper couldn't say what. Moon's boots struck the shallow front steps.

"Anybody home?"

"Just a minute," Jewel called from the kitchen. "I'm coming." She hurried into the room, pushing a strand of hair back from her forehead, leaving behind a white smudge of flour. She wiped her hands on her apron and reached for the brass knob.

"Oh, Moon! What a wonderful surprise! When did you get home?"

Moon ducked his head, embarrassed, as always, in her presence.

"This morning."

"Come in, come in! Walter and Shorty are out in the orchard, spraying for rust mite, but Harper's here."

Moon looked down at his muddy boots. He shook his head, shifting from one foot to the other, then looked away, out past the foothills toward the mountains. "Can't stay. Just stopped by. Say hello to Harper, and you, and . . ."

"Never mind the mud, for heaven's sake!" Jewel said.

"I can clean that up in a minute. And we haven't seen you since—when? November?"

Moon hesitated. He wiped his feet on the grass, then reluctantly stepped inside, looking around, as a stranger might, at the big high-ceilinged room with Jewel's knitting in its basket near the chair by the stove, and the worn rug, and the piano with its clutter of music and books.

From his bed Harper reached out a hand, grinning up at him, "Hey! How come you're home?"

Moon shook his hand, then took off his cap. Harper studied his face. There was the same coarse shock of dark hair, the high cheekbones; the same Moon as ever—a little thinner, perhaps, if that was possible; older, somehow. But something else, something new, a thin line, red as an earthworm, trailing up from his left eye toward his forehead. Moon moved his fingers across his face, then held out his hand for Harper's viewing. An object the size of a coat button lay in his open palm. Red squiggly lines crosshatched its milky surface. From the center of a blue iris, a dark pupil glistened.

Harper swallowed hard. He looked at Moon's face, seeing the slit where the eye had been. A drop of liquid slid from the opening, trembling out of the corner, slowly making its way down his cheek. Moon wiped at it with the rough edge of his sleeve.

"Oh, Moon," Jewel said. She touched his arm. "I'm sorry. . . ."

"What happened?" Harper asked. It was hard to say the words.

With the same quick gesture as before Moon replaced

the eye. It gave a soft squishing plop, then settled into place.

"Fell."

Harper and Jewel waited but Moon seemed to think he'd finished his explanation.

"Must have been some fall," Harper said, trying to sound matter-of-fact, but hollow voiced, feeling sick at his stomach.

"Army doctor give me this glass one. He says I good as new, but they don't want me now."

Jewel shivered. "Moon . . . Moon . . . I'm so . . . sorry." She tried to smile. "But we're glad to have you back, safe, anyway." She shivered again. "Goodness! It's cold, standing here! I'd better get back to the kitchen and check the stove. We want you to stay for supper, so after you finish visiting with Harper, go say hello to the men. I know they'll want to see you. Tell them supper'll be ready in about an hour."

"Yes," said Harper. "Stay. Please stay."

Moon shook his head. "I tell them hello, then be going." He stood for a moment, twisting his cap.

"What you doing in bed?" Moon asked finally. "Got the flu?"

Harper blushed. He wouldn't want Moon to know about his foolishness with the tractor. He shook his head and tried to grin. "Fell."

Moon continued the game. "Must have been some fall!" He started to put on his cap, then dug into his pocket and pulled out a little box. He handed it to Harper. "Brought you somethin'."

"What is it?"

Moon shrugged. "Open it."

Harper lifted the lid. Inside, lying on a satin bed, was a medal with a blue-and-gold-and-red ribbon. He picked it up. The medal was bronze, octagonal in shape, showing an eagle, its wings raised, standing on a globe.

"It's beautiful! Where'd you get it?"

Moon shrugged again.

"Gee! Thanks!"

Moon put his cap on.

"Moon . . ." There was so much to say. He wanted to ask him about the medal. No, that wasn't it. He wanted to ask him about the feather and the tiny package. No. Not that, either. He wanted to warn him about the sheriff. But why would he need to warn him? Moon hadn't done anything wrong. . . . "Moon—wait!"

But Moon was already gone, closing the door behind him. His boots crunched on the gravel path leading around the house. The back gate squeaked open. A few seconds later it banged shut.

Harper could hear Jewel in the kitchen. She'd be standing at the window, he knew, watching Moon's thin back as he followed the path down the meadow to the footbridge across the creek, past the alders and the packing shed, toward the distant line of prune trees where the men were working.

He heard her returning footsteps, and the rustle of her dress. She entered the living room and stood by his bed.

"Poor boy. Losing an eye."

"I'll bet the Japs did it," Harper said. He hated the Japs for that. He fingered the medal. "I'll bet he's a hero."

Jewel stared off in silence, her hand smoothing the bed covers, watching the clouds work their way east. She shook her head. "I don't know what happened. But I do know he didn't lose his eye fighting the Japanese."

"What do you mean?"

Jewel clasped her hands together, as if to stop them from their restless smoothing. "Nettie. You know how she is, the first to hear everything. She said he never left Fort Lewis. The army was going to send him down to Fort Ord, in California, but he didn't go. Some accident, she thought. The army hushed it up. After that, they kept him at Fort Lewis until they could get him a discharge. . . ."

"Why didn't you *tell* me!" That wasn't fair of her, not telling him things like that. He wasn't a child!

Jewel unclasped her hands and began worrying at her wedding ring. "I'm sorry. I really am. I—don't know why. You know how it is with Nettie. A person can't believe half of what she says. I guess I put the whole thing out of my mind. Maybe I didn't want to believe it."

Harper shifted, trying to find a comfortable position. His cast itched. He wished he could scratch. He looked again at the medal, feeling the heavy, solid heft of it in his hand. He could still hear the sucking sound the eye had made when Moon returned it to its socket.

"What about this medal?"

Jewel shrugged. "I don't know."

"Maybe he was doing something brave and fell."

Jewel gave a short, bitter laugh. "There's lots of ways to fall. A fight. A little too much to drink. But I don't remember anybody ever getting a medal for falling."

There was a long pause. Then she sighed. "I know how you care for Moon. I—love him too, I expect. Certainly it's something far stronger than sympathy I feel toward him. There's a fineness in him; a dignity. But there's something about him I don't understand, a strangeness, something I haven't understood since he was just a little boy. Sometimes—and I know this sounds silly—he almost frightens me, though I couldn't say why. . . . You ask about the medal. I don't know how he got it. Perhaps he found it. It's just one more mystery." She laughed, embarrassed. "Listen to me, rattling on this way."

They were both quiet, hearing the sounds of the house; the solemn ticking of the clock, the small clicking scurrying oven noises. The kitchen range needed more wood. Upstairs, a window sash rattled.

"I've got to get back to fixing supper," Jewel said. "The men'll be coming in soon." She turned to go. "I don't know what it is," she said, "but something's bothering me."

"About Moon, you mean?"

She shook her head. "No. Not exactly. I don't know. . . . I keep having the feeling something awful's going to happen. Maybe it's the war. It makes everything seem scary. Even Moon." She gave another short laugh. "Remember last winter—and you back home safe, after worrying us sick, and the sheriff coming, and all? I'm starting to talk like that again."

She left the room. He heard the rattle of the stove lid, and the thump and hiss as she added damp wood to the kitchen fire.

He began cutting out the balsa wood parts he needed for the fuselage. But after a few minutes he pushed the work board down to the side of his bed and looked out the window. The late afternoon sun illuminated a high bank of purple clouds in the east, and the dying light cast a brilliant rosy glow over a small section of the Blue Mountains. The snow was nearly gone from the western slopes. Shouldn't be long now before a person would be able to get in as far as Olinger's. There was something waiting up there, he was sure of that. If he only knew where to look. And wasn't stuck in this cast. And had the courage to go.

A log shifted and settled itself into a new position in the granite stove. He looked around the comfortable room: Walter's paintings, a crock of pussy willows next to the window, the Pendleton blanket with its tan-and-orange-and-scarlet zigzagged Indian weavings thrown over the cane-backed sofa, the Persian rug, threadbare from wear. He raised a hand to his face, pressing hard against one eye, and looked again. All the same. Nothing changed. But at the same time changed completely; the scene flattened, part of its life gone.

He took his hand away. Good smells wafted in from the kitchen: roast beef, cinnamon, onions. . . . Jewel had begun to whistle again; "Love's Old Sweet Song," the sound melancholy and subdued.

Soon the men would be at the back porch, stamping their boots before coming inside. There'd be supper—his on a tray in bed. They'd have told Moon about the sheriff, he bet.

Maybe Moon would stay for supper, and there'd be talk, and some of those questions of his would be answered.

No. That wouldn't happen. Moon would be gone. Gone without a trace, like steam from a kettle. Still, he bet Moon had laughed to himself when they told him about the sheriff.

Sheriffs, he had a hunch, didn't mean a heck of a lot to Moon.

18

Prisoners

A week after Moon's visit, Harper got his cast off. His legs looked pale and thin, and the first day he had to learn to walk all over again. But, oh, the pure bliss: to itch and be able to scratch! For the first three days back at school, Jewel drove him there in the Oldsmobile, but after that he began riding his bike. Two weeks later, on a Friday afternoon after school, he rode down to Lees's Market with Ernie and Jimmy. Ernie said he'd treat—"To celebrate our graduation from this dump!"

Lees's Market was a low white stuccoed building with glass-paned doors opening onto a cool dark interior. Rhubarb, lettuce, onions, and last fall's apples were arranged on a stand under a faded canvas awning in front of the store, next to a gas pump with a flying horse painted on its metal case. Mr. Lees was watering down the gravel to settle the dust as they rode up. The air smelled of hot asphalt and wet gravel and gasoline. He pulled a bandana out of his overalls and wiped the top of his balding head as they rode up. "Boy! It's hot!" he said. "Bet you boys are thirsty! Must be ninety in the shade. I wouldn't be surprised we'll get some good thundershowers later tonight."

Pop bottles stood in the icy water of the big white cooler, their caps shiny in the shadowy light. "I just put a whole new case in. Better feel around to make sure you got a cold one—say, you hear the news? They got Olinger's murderer."

"What?" Harper said.

"That's right. And guess who it is?—Moon! You know who I mean—the guy that lost his eye? Heard it on the radio, not half an hour ago. Caught him red-handed, up at Olinger's place, asleep on the floor inside the cabin. Had Olinger's watch stuffed in his coat pocket. Pretty nervy!"

Harper couldn't move. It wasn't true! It couldn't be true!

"You don't say!" Ernie pulled a nickel and a dime out of his pocket and handed the coins to Mr. Lees. "You two get what you want?" Ernie took a swig of root beer and wiped his mouth with his shirttail. "Don't surprise me a bit. Why, I'll bet that watch is worth maybe fifty bucks! Solid gold! And I'll bet Olinger had money buried away too. Probably some place under the floor. What else did you hear?"

"It was the Umatilla County sheriff caught him. He'd got a tip that Moon was up there, so him and his deputy sneaked up, surrounded the cabin. Said Moon didn't put up any fight. But he wouldn't talk, either. Not a word. They charged him with a whole bunch of things; breaking and entering, theft. But murder's the big one. Brought him down to Pendleton, stuck him in jail." Mr. Lees went inside to put the money in the cash register.

"Moon wouldn't kill anybody! And he wouldn't steal anything, either!" Harper's voice cracked. His mouth was dry. He was starting to sweat under his arms.

Ernie shrugged. "They caught him with the watch, didn't they?"

"So what if they did? Maybe Olinger gave it to him."

"Oh, sure! 'Here, take my watch!' Listen! Moon's crazy! Everybody knows that. That's how come they threw him out of the army. Got in a fight and lost an eye. I hear when he gets mad he just goes crazy. Ain't that right, Jimmy?"

"You take that back!" Harper shouted.

"Take what back?"

"What you said! Moon's *not* crazy!"

Ernie jutted out his jaw. "I'm not takin' nothin' back. He's crazy. He's a crazy, thieving murderer. The sheriff's got the evidence. Now, you want to make something of it?"

Harper could feel the corners of his mouth twitching. "He's not a murderer! And he's not crazy!" He swung his fist, a wild, windmilling swing that struck Ernie squarely on the chin, knocking him in a sprawl against the white enameled side of the cooler. Ernie was up, quick as a cat. He grabbed Harper and threw him to the ground, pressing

Harper's face into the gravel. Harper's mouth filled with dust. Ernie shoved his knee into Harper's back and pinned his arm against his shoulder blade.

"Say Moon's a crazy murderer," Ernie said.

Harper could hardly breathe. His teeth crunched bits of gravel. His ears were ringing. He thought his arm would snap at any moment. He shook his head. No.

"Say it! Murderer! Murderer!"

Ernie shoved harder. Harper shook his head again. He started to cough.

"Hey! What's going on here! Break it up!"

Mr. Lees grabbed Ernie by the shoulder.

"Ah, we was just having a little fun!" said Ernie. "Harper here took a punch at me. I was just showing him who's boss."

"You boys know I won't stand any horsin' around here. Now, settle down." Mr. Lees turned on the hose and recommenced his watering.

Harper stood up, coughing. His right arm burned where Ernie had twisted it. His lip was bleeding. Ernie slapped the dust from his back. "You okay? Here! Drink your pop. Maybe you swallowed a little dust."

They finished their sodas in silence, Harper's hand shaking so that he could scarcely hold the bottle. Ernie cleared his throat. "Well, I've got to be getting home," he said lamely. "Chores."

"Yeah, me too," Jimmy said.

"Well, see you Monday," Ernie said to Harper. "See you, Mr. Lees."

Harper set his bottle down beside the crate. Still not

looking at either one of them, he climbed on his bike and started for home. His lower lip was puffing out like a piece of liver. It wasn't true! He knew it wasn't true! He'd crossed the railroad tracks and passed Ed Weed's weathered packing shed when he heard the squeak and rattle of a bicycle behind him.

"Hey!"

He glanced back. It was Ernie, standing up, pumping hard, grinning at him. "You socked me a good one!"

Ernie pulled alongside. There was a long silence. "Moon's my friend," Harper said finally, his voice shaking. He was afraid he'd start to cry right on the spot. "He's been my friend a long time."

"Yeah . . . I know. I forgot, I guess—how's your lip?"

Harper's eyes stayed fixed to the road. "It's okay—how's your chin?"

"Ah, who needs a chin!" There was another silence. "Anyway—see you Monday!" Ernie turned and rode away.

Harper stood up on the pedals and started pumping. Heat waves shimmered like water on the road. On his right, Frank Demaris was mowing his first cutting of hay, his ancient green-and-yellow John Deere tractor clattering across a sea of alfalfa. On his left a robin alighted on a fence post, then changed its mind and bobbed clumsily across Henry Hoffman's pasture.

What a crazy world, where a person could feel mad and sad and bewildered and proud and anxious and worried sick all at the same time!

* * *

Later, after a solemn supper, Harper slouched down to the creek. The evening sun was casting long yellow summery shadows, and the Horse Heaven Hills lay in gold-and-purple folds. Above them clouds were beginning to form. Mr. Lees might be right; the air had that hush that precedes a thundershower. From the distance came the bellow of Dickerson's big penned-up holstein bull. Pulling off his shoes and socks, Harper waded through a tangle of buttercups and pale blue forget-me-nots into the icy water, picking up rocks, searching for flat ones to skip. A pennywinkle—a stone fly larva—had built its house on the underside of one rock. Harper pried the little cylindrical house loose and began peeling back the walls of tiny brightly colored pebbles. The builder, a fat yellow grub with a black head and whiskers, appeared, clinging tenaciously to what wall remained.

Impulsively, Harper gave the grub a toss. It arced through the air and landed downstream at the end of the little pool where Moon had launched his silky-sailed ship, so long ago. There was a dark shadow, a boil of water, and a snap, and the grub was gone.

Standing motionless in the cold stream, Harper caught his breath. He hadn't meant to do that. Stone fly larvae made terrific bait—Olinger would have scorned them!—but they were the best you could find; they even obligingly curled themselves into neat little whorls as if inviting one to impale them on a hook. Trout loved them.

But this larva, now, seemed—different. Looking down, Harper saw the ruin of its house pasted against the edge of a rock under six inches of water. He dislodged it with a toe and watched as it floated away, bumping against first one rock and then another, until it too disappeared into the depths of the pool, glassy smooth in the evening light.

He wished he could run these last three minutes backward, so the water would boil and the pennywinkle would pop out of the pool into his hand, and the little pebbled rind would wind itself whole again, with the owner safe and cozy and snug inside its tiny house.

But that wouldn't happen. Time moves in one direction only.

Slowly he made his way to shore. He sat down, rubbing his icy feet against the grass to wipe them dry, staring off past the creek at the dark orchard and the rosy evening sky. The alder stirred and shook its leaves. The clouds were forming fast, now.

What—who was a prisoner, anyway? Take this afternoon. Supposing he'd done what Ernie asked, and said that Moon was a murderer? Would that have made him less Ernie's prisoner? Or more? It seemed like an unanswerable question.

Or the stone fly grub. You'd think for sure it was a prisoner, spending its days locked up in its little spit-and-pebble jail. But set it free, and the next thing you know, a trout's eating supper.

A hummingbird darted past in the darkening air and landed on a thistle just beginning to crown. Harper shivered, half expecting a young Moon to appear, clutching a wooden ship to the bib of his ragged overalls.

How could they even think of locking up Moon! Why,

that would be like locking up a—a hummingbird or the creek or a cloud! Lock Moon up, and he'd die! Besides, he was innocent. Harper was as sure of that as he was of his own name. He didn't care what Ernie or Mr. Lees or any of them said. And he'd prove it too somehow.

He sat down on the grassy bank and rubbed his toes dry, then began putting on his socks. He hadn't practiced the piano yet, and he still had a page of arithmetic to do.

In the middle of lacing up his shoes, he stopped short. What if he was wrong, and Ernie and the rest of them were right? The sheriff wouldn't have arrested Moon unless he had some pretty good evidence, would he? What about the watch? And Olinger's body, half buried under a pile of fir needles and moss? And the feathers in the dead man's hand? Somebody did those things.

And if not Moon, then who? Buck? Jeeter? Not on your life! They were too dumb to do anything that . . . complicated.

Maybe jail was where Moon belonged; locked up where he couldn't hurt anybody, including himself.

No. No! He hated himself for even thinking the thought! Jewel was right. There *was* a kind of strangeness in Moon; a difference. But not frightening. More a sort of—distance, almost as if Moon were—what? A visitor from another time? Another world? "No man is an island unto himself," Mrs. Emory, his teacher, was fond of saying. But he doubted if she'd ever known Moon.

He stood up and started for the house. That's when he saw the cloud of dust. It was the sheriff's car, driving in the lane.

19

Armed and Dangerous

Harper could hear the first far-off grumblings of thunder as he rounded the house. The sheriff was making his way up the walk. The door opened, and Walter stood on the front step. The sheriff lifted a hand in greeting. Walter nodded.

"I wondered if I might talk to you."

"I don't know why not," Walter said.

The sheriff took off his campaign hat and patted the sweat from his freckled forehead with a folded handkerchief. "Pretty good spell of weather."

Walter nodded. "I doubt that's why you're here."

The sheriff flushed. "We got off on the wrong foot last time." He fanned himself with his campaign hat. "And I probably had the biggest part in it—mind if I sit down?" He indicated the broad step. "I guess you know we brought Moon in yesterday."

Walter nodded.

The sheriff seated himself. Harper joined his father, still standing.

"We found him up at Olinger's—me and Elmer Pascavis—he's my deputy. There wasn't no rough stuff, mind you. We never laid a finger on him, either one of us, except to search him. And he didn't try to get away. He had the watch on him. Funny thing—he was asleep and all—but it almost seemed like he was expecting us."

"So?"

The sheriff laid his hat to one side. "Anyway, this morning, when Elmer went in to wake him up and give him his rations, the door was unlocked—well, not exactly unlocked, but I'll get to that later—and Moon was gone."

"You mean he'd escaped?" Harper asked. "But the radio said . . ."

"That's because I haven't let it out yet that he's gone. I didn't want to stir things up, you understand. You know how people can get all worked up when there's a prisoner on the loose. Anyway, the blanket was propped up with a pillow and all bunched together, so's it looked like he was sleeping."

Walter lowered himself to the step. Harper did the same.

"How'd he get out?" Harper asked. The thunder clapped, closer this time, and a light breeze swept the lawn, stirring the maple pods that lay on the grass.

The sheriff grimaced. "He must have done it himself. The whole goldarned locking mechanism was gone. Everything. Clean as a whistle. And it wasn't just some simple little lock and key, you know what I mean? Why, it'd take a locksmith half a day with special tools to get that thing out of there. And Elmer, out front at the desk, all night long, where you'd think he'd hear if there was something fishy going on."

"Why are you telling us this?" Walter asked.

The sheriff studied one of his ancient polished boots, then flicked off a speck of dust that Harper couldn't see. "You know, that first time when we talked, me and the boy here, Harper, I guess I pretty well had my mind made up about what went on up there at Olinger's. Now, well, I'm not so sure."

"Why not?"

"I don't believe I'm in an official position to say right now. We need to take a look at some peculiarities in the case. I'll be getting Doc Haney—he's Umatilla County coroner—up there in a day or two to take a look at the body. That ought to help give us a better picture of what happened. Now don't get me wrong. I'm not backing off. I still think Moon's behind all this, you understand. But I want to get the facts straight. That's only fair. And right now, I've got an escaped prisoner on my hands; one who's charged with murder." The sheriff hesitated. "But that's not all."

"What else?"

"He took a rifle with him."

Walter bristled. "You mean you left unprotected arms lying around?"

"No, sir! Not unprotected! Locked up in a solid walnut

case, along with half a dozen others! Not twenty feet from where Elmer was sitting! And him swearing up and down he didn't close an eye all night long. But the lock was open, and a rifle gone—just a little thing; an old twenty-two caliber single shot—and a box of shells. Why Moon'd take that particular rifle, I don't know. It was a piece of junk. We had some beautiful guns in there. Guns we'd confiscated."

"So what are you going to do?" Walter asked.

"Do? Why, the only thing I can do. Find him. Bring him back. That's why I'm here, telling you. I know he's got no family, but from what I hear, you folks are probably as close to him as anyone. Especially the boy. And I don't have a doubt in my mind he's either headed back to Olinger's, or bound this way. I figger he's got a hideout somewhere in the neighborhood." He turned suddenly to Harper. "You know where it is?"

Harper remembered last winter; all the fruitless searching. "No, sir."

"You sure?"

Harper nodded.

The sheriff reached for his hat. "That's what I was afraid of."

A strange yellow light filled the sky, and the thunder clapped and rolled again, closer this time. The storm was coming up fast.

"Damn it, man!" the sheriff said, getting to his feet and looking at Walter, who had also risen. "Don't you see? I'm trying to tell you I need your help, and it's not easy.

We've got to get Moon back. For God's sake, he's charged with theft and murder, not to mention breaking and entering! It's your duty, if you hear of him, or if he tries to get in touch with Harper here, to call me. So far as I'm concerned, he's armed and dangerous. To all of us. To himself.''

20

The Cellar

Harper woke from a troubled sleep, his heart racing. He was late. He'd have to hurry. He threw the covers back and lay as straight as he could on the damp sheets, his body sticky with sweat, his mouth dry, staring up at the ceiling, trying to calm himself. Late for what? He didn't have to go anywhere.

He got out of bed and peered out the open window. Not a light in sight. The storm had passed quickly, but the wind had knocked down a power line earlier, and it looked as if the electricity was still off. The air was cool and smelled of sagebrush and damp earth and wet hay. Water dripped lazily from the eave of the roof. Great clouds rolled across the sky, bright stars glittering behind them. Faint and far off, toward the east, he could hear the brooding grumble of distant thunder. A faint golden glow silhouetted the dark line of the Blue Mountains. There'd be a moon later.

Moon! That's what had waked him. He had to go to Moon. But where?

"Oh, come on!" he heard a voice inside himself saying. "You know where. You've always known! No-Man's-Land. That's where! That's why you never looked there. Because you didn't want to know. But now you've got to. You've got to warn him. Now! Go now! And don't trust the stairs! And don't try to explain it to Mom and Dad! Climb out the window onto the porch. And hurry!"

Reluctantly, he pulled on his corduroys and jersey, careful to be as quiet as possible. He felt around on the floor for his socks and sneakers. He'd carry them until he was off the roof. His footing would be better that way.

Wait. He'd better take a candle. And matches. There they were, next to the clock. He'd brought them upstairs last night, after the lights went out, to light his way to bed.

He climbed out the window, reaching with one toe as far as he could until he touched the roof shingles. The rain had made them slippery, and for one heart-stopping second he almost lost his footing. A loose shingle slithered down the porch roof and fell to the ground, landing with a soft plop. He waited, half in and half out the window, for some clue that Walter or Jewel had heard. But all was silent. He tossed his sneakers onto the grass. A second later, he jumped.

Hurriedly, he pulled on his socks and laced up his sneakers. He wheeled his bike up the little rise of the lane before getting on. His right pedal squeaked, but once he was away from the house no one would recognize the sound. When he reached the end of the lane he turned left.

He passed the schoolhouse and Stinnet's gas station and Whipple's house and the corner where the road branched south to the farm labor camp. No-Man's-Land loomed ahead. He could make out the sagging roof of the dilapidated barn, and the silhouette of scraggly pines against the horizon. He wheeled his bike to the side of the road and left it there. He'd walk the rest of the way.

At the entrance to the yew-lined lane, he stood for a moment, waiting, trying to get up enough nerve to enter. Once he thought he caught a glimpse of something behind him, down the road, the way he'd come. He watched, trying to see if it moved. It didn't. He must have been wrong.

Well, no use putting off going in any longer. The yews closed about him after his first few steps, and then the abandoned house loomed up, dark and ominous, under its canopy of Norwegian maples. It was the house that held the secret, if there was a secret. He crept around the side of it like a blind man, shuffling his feet to keep from stumbling, one hand tracing his way along the alligatored wood siding. His foot struck the rough mortared stone sides of the cellar entrance and he lost his balance and nearly fell. He reached down, feeling more than seeing the cellar door itself. If he could get into the cellar, there might be steps back up into the house itself.

The cellar entrance was slanted so rain wouldn't gather and run down there. He gave the door handle a tug. Just as he'd thought; it didn't move. Certainly it had been years since it had been opened. He pulled again, harder this time. Suddenly—so suddenly he tumbled over backward—the door opened, then fell shut again with a loud thud.

He scrambled to his feet, his whole body trembling.

Somebody was down there! That's why the door had opened.

Nonsense! It was just an old door, that's all. Old nails. The wood rotting away. Crazy, how a person starts imagining things!

He pulled on the handle again, hinges creaking, the wood splintered and rough. A spider web caught across his face and he jerked his hand up to brush it away. He tried to peer down into the darkness. Wished it wasn't so dark. He dreaded going down those stairs. There'd be black widows there, for sure.

Come on! Come on! Get it over with!

He laid the door flat against the mortared sidewall and started down the packed earth stairs. At the bottom was another door. He shoved against it. It gave way, and he stepped inside, feeling the irregular earthen floor under his feet. There was a mingling of smells; moldy fruit and sauerkraut and damp earth and another smell—a wild, acrid, metallic smell he knew but didn't want to name.

He lit his candle. He was in a small root cellar; the board ceiling not six feet high, the walls of packed earth, two of them fronted with sagging old shelves, littered with junk, a can of rusty nails, old pipe joints, an ax head, a set of old spark plugs, empty beer bottles, a hammer, gopher and mousetraps, scraps of angle iron. In one corner were several old stone crocks, in another a rusting cream separator and an equally rusted pick and shovel. Dusty jars of fruit and vegetables, their tops covered with gray mold, stood in scattered ranks on the shelves. Some of the jars had burst open, and bits of glass and fruit lay spewed on the floor. But that had happened a long time ago; the fruit was dried, the glass particles covered with grime.

The back wall, the one facing him, had a board running its length, measured off with wooden pegs from which hung all sorts of things; a horse collar, a broken washboard, drawers from a cabinet, a couple of old lanterns, broken picture frames, worn-out picking sacks, a dark green oil slicker. In one corner hung a faded canvas tarpaulin, stiff with dirt.

He drew the tarpaulin aside a few inches. What was this! Behind the heavy canvas, in the shadows, was what appeared to be another door; two faded green boards, each over a foot wide, fastened together with rough one-by-six boards, and reaching from floor to ceiling. On one side, he could see the backs of rusted hinges.

Perhaps it was a cupboard. But why wasn't there a handle of some kind? And if it was a cupboard, why cover it with a tarp? And who ever heard of a person embedding a cupboard in what seemed to be a dirt wall? None of it made sense.

But he wasn't going to stop now. Using a beer bottle for a holder, he set the candle on a shelf. A few seconds later, with the hammer as a pry, he had the door open. Holding the candle high, he looked inside. But the cupboard, if it was a cupboard, was empty, lacking even shelves. The cupboard backing was two green boards, similar to the front.

Wait a minute. Look at this hook. The door was fastened on the inside. That's what held the cabinet shut. But why would anybody want to fasten a cabinet door on the inside? They'd have to be inside to fasten it. And there wasn't that much. . . .

He knocked on the green-board backing. It resonated like a drum.

There was another room behind the boards! There had to be!

He shoved with his shoulder at the cupboard back, feeling it give. He shoved again. With a sudden clatter the boards moved inward. That faint, acrid, sweet, metallic odor—that odor he knew but wouldn't name—hung in the air, mingled with the friendlier smells of tobacco smoke and turpentine and paint.

It was a tiny room, perhaps eight feet long and six feet wide, hollowed out of the earth and daubed white with calcimine. A narrow cot covered with a quilt stood against one earthen wall, a muddy combat boot next to it. An overturned kitchen chair lay on the packed dirt floor next to the other wall. At the far end of the room was a rude workbench littered with tin cans, bottle corks, bits of glass, bark, twine, twists of coarse grass, a jar of brushes, a glue pot, and cans of paint. Big cardboard boxes were stacked under the bench. The candle's flickering light revealed shadowy faces staring at him from a shelf out of the darkness above the bench: Walter, Jewel, Shorty, Olinger . . . himself.

Then, looking down, he saw the bare foot and a ragged trouser cuff; the coarse shock of black hair; the long, yellowed, pale face; the slack mouth; the khaki shirt, with a glaze of thick red blood oozing from it onto the earthen floor. Moon! Somebody'd killed Moon!

He sank to his knees and grabbed Moon's wrist. It was still warm. He tried to find a pulse but couldn't.

He shoved the candle close to Moon's open mouth. For a long second the flame was steady. Then it flickered. It grew steady again. Then flickered once more.

Below him, Moon's body began to jerk and twist. "No! Ma! No!" he pleaded, his voice that of a four-year-old. He drew up his legs as if to protect himself. His arms flailed about. His eyes flew open and he gazed wildly about the room, his face distorted with fear; blood and saliva seeped from his mouth. Harper knelt beside him, striking his knee hard against something.

"Moon!" he said. "It's me! Harper!"

The flailing stopped. Moon squinted at him. Finally, his face twisted in a ghost of the old grin. He tried to speak. Harper bent over to hear him, his ear to Moon's mouth.

"Bum shot," Moon said, his voice a faint whisper.

Then Harper saw what it was his knee had struck; the thin butt of a cheap old .22 rifle.

21

Fair and Square

Moon was in Saint Mary's Hospital in less than an hour. Harper had roused Mr. Whipple, the closest neighbor, and they'd rushed him to town on a makeshift bed in the back of Whipple's pickup. Two days later Moon was taken off the critical list, and the doctor said his chances of recovery were good. But Harper had found him just in time, the doctor added; half an hour later and Moon would have died for certain from loss of blood.

That evening while the family was finishing supper the sheriff's car pulled in the lane and parked under the maple trees. The sheriff got out, a small bouquet in his hand, and walked up the brick path to the house. The front door was open.

"Anybody home?" he called.

"Come in," Walter said, standing at the door. He held out his hand. The sheriff shook it, then repeated the ceremony with Shorty and Harper. "I—uh—brought some flowers for the missus."

"Maybe you'd like a cup of coffee," Walter said.

"That'd be nice."

A few minutes later they were all seated around the table. The sheriff cleared his throat. "Well, let me start right off by saying that I made a pretty good mess of this case early on. Thank God things turned out like they did. If it hadn't been for young Harper here, we'd be a sorry group."

He stirred his coffee and took a sip.

"I got the coroner's report yesterday. According to Doc Haney, Olinger's death was caused by a 'thrombus in the left anterior descending coronary.' That's a heart attack. The wound on his forehead was probably caused by a fall, maybe at the same time or even earlier, but there was no evidence of foul play. So that takes care of the murder charge."

The sheriff straightened the ribbon on his campaign hat. "According to what I can figure out—Moon helped me with some of this, and he's not a big talker, as I guess you know—the same day Olinger died Moon hiked up to tell him good-bye because he was leaving for the army. When he got there, he found Olinger laying dead on the floor of the cabin. He didn't want to leave the body like that, naturally, but he didn't have much time if he was going to beat the storm back down the mountain, so he made a quick job of it and buried him shallow, intending to come back later and do the job proper. That make sense to you?" He looked around the table.

They nodded. "But what about the watch?" Harper asked, dreading to hear the answer.

The sheriff was silent for a moment before answering. "I asked Moon about that, hoping he'd say Olinger had given it to him. But he wouldn't."

Jewel shook her head and smiled. "That sounds just like Moon. If Olinger gave him the watch, he'd say so. If he didn't, he wouldn't. Moon doesn't lie."

"I'm beginning to find that out," the sheriff said wryly. "Anyway, from what I gather, Moon took the watch before he buried him. He thought a lot of Olinger, and the old man felt the same way about him. I can't say I blame him for taking it—a keepsake, if you know what I mean—I wonder if I might have a little warm-up on that coffee?"

Harper pushed his chair back. "I'll get it."

The sheriff nodded his thanks. There was another silence, longer this time.

"There's just a couple more things, then I'll be out of your hair. I called Fort Lewis to check on Moon's service record. That decoration he brought home? You remember? It was his all right, fair and square. It's called the Soldier's Medal. It's the highest award you can get for bravery outside of combat. I've sent for a copy of the citation. I'll see you get one."

The sheriff stirred his coffee, laid down the spoon; straightened it, laid it down again. "Seems that while Moon was on maneuvers with his company, they'd stopped for noon mess and a troop carrier broke loose and started down the hill straight toward them. Moon was sitting to one side. A loner, like always, I guess. He seen the thing comin'; grabbed up a big fallen tree branch, and using it as a kind of wedge, threw himself straight in the way of that big truck, causing it to turn enough so's it rolled down a ravine without hurting a soul." The sheriff paused. He picked up the troublesome spoon, turned it over in his hands. "Excepting that Moon fell, and got poked in the eye with a stick."

There was a long, long silence. "Thank you, Sheriff," Jewel said finally.

The sheriff put the spoon down and reached for his hat. "Well, that about sums it up." He coughed into his fist. "I—uh—wonder if I might just ask a favor of you folks? Then I'll be on my way."

"What'd you have in mind?" That was Walter.

The sheriff turned his campaign hat in his hands, rubbing at an invisible spot on the brim. "Well," he said finally, "it's like this. Just looking at the evidence, you might conclude that Moon tried to shoot himself in the heart. If someone's using a rifle instead of a pistol, that's one way he might do it. Take off a shoe and sock, sit on a chair, aim, pull the trigger with a bare toe. Now, I know when Harper found Moon, he had one of his boots off and all. But who knows? Maybe he was getting ready for bed."

The sheriff hesitated. "People are funny. You know what I mean? They think somebody's tried to kill himself, they could hold it against him. I'm writing this whole thing up as an accident, and if it's all the same to you folks, I'd suggest you think of it the same way. Guns do have a habit of going off all by themselves, now and then. Sometimes when least expected."

22

Saint Mary's

Saturday afternoon Jewel and Walter and Shorty drove to Saint Mary's Hospital for visiting hours. Harper wouldn't go. He kept seeing Moon's long bare foot, and the .22 rifle, and the dark stain of blood on the packed earth cellar floor. Or Moon's body, drawn and twisted like a beaten child's.

He didn't want to see those things. He wanted to see Moon as he'd been when he was young, loping across the pasture, grinning a greeting, packing along some strange new thing he'd found; the bone white skull of a mouse, a tiny basket woven from grass and straw, a genuine agate, a ship he'd carved from a peach pit.

Sunday passed, and Monday. At last, on Tuesday afternoon, when the farm was listless with summer heat, he stuffed a candle and matches in his pocket. All right, he told himself, he'd go to Saint Mary's, just for a minute. But first, he'd stop at No-Man's-Land. Maybe there were some answers there.

The lane leading into the little gray house was dim with whispering shadows. The air smelled of rotting toadstools. The slanting cellar-door entrance, rising up from the ground like a rude sarcophagus, was padlocked shut. A notice signed by the sheriff declared the premises off-limits.

He found a screwdriver in the tumbledown barn and unscrewed the hinges to the cellar door, careful not to damage the notice. He lifted the door and closed it behind him. The air was damp and close and smelled of mice and spoiled fruit and a lingering, faint, acrid odor of gunpowder. He lighted a candle and made his way down the rough stairs and through the cupboard opening into Moon's small whitewashed room. A kerosene lantern stood on the workbench. He lighted it and adjusted the wick.

The calcimined walls glowed with light. The faces stared down at him: Jewel, Walter, Shorty, Olinger, himself. After a moment's hesitation he reached up for the one of Olinger.

The curious thing was how, at a distance, it *was* Olinger; one could smell the old man's smell of tobacco and sweat and neat's-foot oil and Smith Brothers cough drops and some undefined underlying mysterious odor of aging; one could see the abstracted glance, as if Olinger was holding on to some private, half-comic, half-tragic thought; one could almost hear Olinger's wheezing chuckle. But what Harper held in his hands was an assemblage of baling wire, thread, yarn, bark, glass shards, newspaper, cloth, and hard wads of chewed gum, daubed together with glue and paint. Olinger had disappeared.

He set the mask back on the shelf. Once again the eyes twinkled, the mouth twisted in an ironic, half-mocking smile.

Uneasily, Harper turned his glance away and studied the rest of the room. Under the workbench, pushed far back and deep in shadow, were battered cardboard boxes—the kind you'd find stacked empty out back of Safeway—Heinz ketchup, Birds Eye peas, Libby tomato juice, Wheaties, Kellogg's cornflakes—the kind of big cardboard boxes Moon might use to make things.

He pulled out a box that had held Del Monte peaches, being careful not to disturb the others. It felt empty, or nearly so. He shook it. No. There was something inside. The top was sealed shut with brown paper tape. "Don't open it," he told himself. "It's none of your business, what's inside that box."

But he had to look. He had to know. He opened his pocketknife and slit the tape, removed the top, and held up the lantern to peer inside.

Disappointment. Inside the box was just another box, not much bigger than a shoe box, and thin wires leading out of it to a flashlight battery and a switch.

He lifted the shoe box out and shifted it around so as to see all sides. What was this? A window. He touched the switch, and peered in. Why, it was his home kitchen! There was the bright red linoleum countertop, and the white refrigerator, and the big shiny black-and-chrome Monarch cook stove, and the glass-fronted dish cupboard. The lamp glowed. It was suppertime. Sitting at the table, under the lamplight, were Jewel and Walter and Shorty and himself. Shorty was drinking coffee out of a saucer. A newspaper lay alongside Walter's chair. Jewel was smoothing back her hair. Harper was balancing peas on a knife.

Nonsense. He was imagining it all. The figures were nothing but bits of string and twists of paper and tinfoil and yarn, touched here and there with dabs of paint.

And besides, there were no doors. There was no way in. He flicked the switch off. The cozy room was gone.

Carefully, he put the box back in place. Should he open another?

Yes. He pulled out the biggest of the boxes, the one that had held a case of Wheaties, slit the paper tape, and peered inside.

It was Olinger's store. Holding the lantern close to the log wall, Harper peered inside through a red-curtained window. There was a half-finished carving on the kitchen table, and the familiar worn sink with the galvanized bucket, and the snowshoes, and Olinger's cot in the corner, and the pile of magazines, and the store counter, and the licorice jar, and the shelves holding tins of sardines and cans of baked beans and bottles of ketchup and mustard. But then he saw something else he'd not noticed before; a meadow, and the dusty road. And Olinger, standing in the doorway, his arms outstretched. And a lanky barefoot boy, running across the meadow toward him.

He caught his breath and closed the top of the box. Enough. He'd seen enough.

No. He'd open one more.

What was this? A miniature Ford delivery wagon, perfectly scaled, the body of painted green tin, and Paddie, spruced up and jaunty, at the wheel. Harper lifted the little truck out of the box and set it on the workbench, almost expecting Paddie to hop out and set up his paints. He opened the cleverly hinged back door—the smells of turpentine and paint and whiskey and lamp oil and smoke!—and saw, in the light of the kerosene lantern, Tessie sitting on her cot, her long braided hair falling down her back, a glass at her elbow, absorbed in the tarot. He could almost see the ringed hands moving, moving over the tiny figured cards.

And what was this, on the floor of the truck? An infant, bound to a board, with a rag across its mouth.

Staring at the scene, Harper had the uneasy feeling he'd invaded something terribly private. What he'd done was not the same as snooping through drawers or peeking into medicine cabinets or reading someone else's mail. Those were harmless small intrusions.

What he'd done was look into Moon's heart, where he had no business looking.

Nonsense! Why, the baby was just a bit of bark, and a thin strip of cloth, and a broken popsicle stick! And Paddie and Tessie were two bits of loosely woven painted wire, clothed with crumples of gauzy tissue and string! The whole thing was nothing more than the harmless play of someone clever with his hands.

But if that's all they were, why did they seem so real?

Suddenly, he couldn't get out fast enough. He closed

the box and sealed it shut. He turned down the lantern wick to extinguish the flame, grabbed the candle, hastened up the stairs, and pushed back the cellar door.

Oh! The outside air was sweet! He could smell wild roses and alfalfa hay and dry locust blossoms. He screwed the door hinges back on the cellar door and flung the screwdriver into the weeds by the side of the house.

When he reached the end of the lane, he looked back, half expecting to see Moon's lanky form, standing there, guarding his secrets. He turned toward home and rode fifty yards or so. Then he stopped. For a long minute he stood astride his bike. Finally, reluctantly, he turned back the way he'd just come and continued on, past No-Man's-Land, across the Walla Walla River bridge, across the Yellow Hawk bridge, past the dizzyingly fragrant onion fields and the ripening wheat fields, past the green lawns of the country club and the dusty grandeur of the fairground pavilion.

Saint Mary's was a huge pile of bricks, dark as blood, the windows and high front door framed in gray granite. The air inside smelled of carbolic acid and formaldehyde and pine soap and rubbing alcohol and iodine and the dread odors of disease and death. Visiting hours had just begun. He climbed the wide worn stone stairs to the second floor, stealing down the hallway like a criminal. Grimy cracks fissured the pea green terrazzo floors. The walls were a sickly blue. Nuns, their pale faces buried deep in starched wimples, their black-and-white garments flapping in an undetected wind, passed him, intent on their mysterious journeys. White-stockinged nurses wearing steel-rimmed glasses and squeaky crepe-soled shoes hurried by. An old man in shapeless overalls dabbed at the floor with a stringy gray mop. Distant fans and motors hummed and whined and clanked.

Moon's room was at the end of the hall; Jewel had told him the number. The varnished door, yellowed with age and grime, was ajar. The room was hushed in a twilight dimness; the venetian blinds covering the tall window were closed shut. Peonies, black from lack of water, stood in a glass jar.

He'd made a mistake. It was the wrong room. The person lying under the bed sheet was too small, too still to be Moon. He turned to leave. He saw the name card in its thin metal frame on the door: JAMES PATRICK MCCARTY.

He hesitated, then crept back, wishing he could run away, not knowing why he'd come.

A heavy glass bottle with red markings hung upside down from a tall stand next to the bed. A tube, pale as tallow, ran from the bottle to a needle inserted into a thin brown arm. Harper slid closer to the bed. He saw Moon's face, gaunt and green in the shadowy light. Moon's one good eye flew open. Harper could feel his gaze full on him. He felt five years old again. He had the feeling that Moon knew everything; knew he'd just come from No-Man's-Land; knew he'd opened the boxes, knew what he'd seen.

He tried to say something. Anything. His tongue was glued tight. He tried to swallow, and couldn't.

"How come you shot yourself?" His voice was harsh as Tessie's.

Moon looked away. There was a long silence. Harper could hear machinery thump, thump, thumping somewhere in the building.

Moon reached under his pillow. He handed a kitchen matchbox—the big kind—to Harper.

"Presen'," he whispered hoarsely.

Harper opened the matchbox. Inside was Moon's whitewashed room. There was the workbench, with the dark shadows beneath, and the shelf with the masks, and the cot. And the lamp. And an open box. And himself, holding Paddie's green truck.

A wave of shame passed over him.

He wanted to reach out, wanted to apologize. What was it about Moon that let him know everything?

"Ah," he said softly, as if to himself. "Ah . . ." His voice trailed off. "Anyway," he said finally, saying surely the most foolish thing anyone had ever said, "we're even, huh?"

Moon reached out and gripped Harper's hand. He smiled weakly and shook his head.

"Brothers," Moon said. "We brothers. Brothers don't keep score."

23

Butterflies

It was August. They were on their way out to the Point, the two of them, kicking loose shale, sauntering along, easy. At the place on the trail where Olinger had always muttered, "Danged knee," Moon reached up toward his face. "Danged eye," he said.

Harper shook his head and grinned.

When they reached the Point, they stood for a moment looking west. It was a clear afternoon, late, and they could see a golden ribbon where the Columbia River made its big bend. The sky was blue and clear with a touch of haze, and the Horse Heaven Hills, tawny in the distance, lay folded in shadow. The air was sweet with the odors of warm dust and warmed stone and tiny shy summer flowers.

"How's it feel? Being a storekeeper?"

Moon shrugged and grinned. He found a flat place on the rocky ledge, sat down, and leaned back. "Guess you hear about sheriff. Bought the place for back taxes. Told me to pay him back when I got the money. Forty-eight more dollars—it be all mine."

There was a long, companionable silence. A cloud's shadow raced across the valley, far below. A red-tailed hawk soared high above them in ever-widening circles. A warm evening breeze danced its way up the rocky slope, bending the dried cheat grass and tiny flowers. An ant wrestling with a twig ten times its size stumbled over the rough shale, stopped briefly to converse with another ant, then scurried on.

Harper looked over at Moon. His face was still thin but brown and healthy-looking. A black patch covered the missing eye.

"How come you don't use the eye the army gave you?"

Moon shrugged. "Don't know. Feel better this way."

Another long silence. Harper picked at a splotch of gray lichen with his fingernail. "Did Olinger ever tell you about that medal of his—the Bronze Star?"

Moon was chewing on a grass stem, gazing at the far-away hills. He nodded.

"What'd he tell you?"

Moon picked up a handful of pebbles and started tossing them, underhanded, at a nearby rock. They'd hit with a ping, and then glance off, one bouncing this way and the next another. For a long time Harper thought he wasn't going to answer.

"Tell me he be sorry forever he have it," Moon said finally, his voice so soft that Harper wasn't sure he'd heard right.

"Why?" he asked. He couldn't believe it.

"You know how he get it?"

"Wiped out a German machine-gun nest, Dad told me, all by himself. Saved his whole squad. Not one German left alive. Isn't that what happened?"

Moon tossed another pebble, carefully, deliberately, as if tossing pebbles was the most interesting and absorbing thing he'd ever done.

"France, last war," he said, almost more to himself than Harper. "World War One. Olinger maybe forty, forty-five. Squad sergeant. His men just kids. Seventeen, eighteen. They call him Pop." Another pebble. "Machine gun open up. No place to hide. Trapped. Don't worry, he tell 'em. Stay where they are. They safe. He be back."

The same ant they'd seen before hurried past, going the other way, waggling its twig like a banner.

"Olinger take his rifle, a couple hand grenades, start out running. Big open field. Little hill off where he think gun is. Noise. Shells whistling. He catch a bullet in his knee. But he keep on running, zigzagging, dragging one leg. He close now. Throw a grenade. Another. Smoke all around. Machine gun stop."

Moon paused.

"And then?"

"He look around. Can't see nothin' at first. Smoke everywhere. Then he see Germans. All dead, next to gun. He hear something, right behind him. Olinger shoot."

Harper tried to swallow. "And?"

"A boy. Drummer boy. Still got his little wooden sticks in his hands. And his drum. He maybe . . . thirteen. Bullet hit him right here."

With his finger, Moon touched Harper's forehead.

It seemed to Harper there was a great awful roaring in his head. Moon tossed the last of his pebbles.

"So that's why he came up here," Harper said, after a long time.

Moon nodded.

They sat for a few minutes longer. "You ready?" Moon asked.

Harper got to his feet. They hiked the first couple hundred yards without saying a word. They left the hard sharp shale behind and entered the first outriding pines. The air was different here, fragrant with the smell of warm resin. The late afternoon sun cast long beams of light. A chipmunk scooted across the path.

"What's that?" Harper said suddenly. For half a second, he'd thought he caught a glimpse of something moving up ahead, where the first of the firs replaced the pines.

"Where?" Moon said.

"There. Over there." It seemed strange to him that Moon hadn't seen it first.

"Don't see anything."

"There! Can't you see it? Right behind that big tree. I thought I saw somebody standing there. . . . probably just imagining things."

The path was climbing now; the trees closer together. The earth was soft underfoot; centuries of green and growing things living out their lives and dying and falling to the ground, making room for more green and growing things.

There! There it was again! Knew he'd seen something! Fluttering, almost like a giant bird, behind the trees. But further off than before. He looked at Moon.

"I see it," Moon said softly.

They stood watching, not daring to move. How could it slip through the branches like that, almost as if the trees weren't there?

Now, where had it gone? For it had disappeared.

No. There it was, straight ahead of them, near the path, only a few hundred feet away, bigger than Harper had at first thought, filmy; and gleaming like silver. It was like looking at some gauzy cloth, dancing and shimmering in the darkening air.

They were walking easily now, hurrying a bit, the path level. Whatever they'd seen had disappeared behind some trees, but that didn't matter. They'd see it again. Although Harper couldn't have said why, he felt a great sense of happiness; lighthearted, the same feeling he always got in the spring, when the thaws started.

Then, halfway to the cabin, they saw it, plain for the first time. Why, it was butterflies! Masses of black-and-gray-and-silvery butterflies, sliding through the trees as effortlessly as moonbeams. Thousands of them, millions of them, their wings slow and indolent, dancing together through the forest.

They were close to the butterflies now, so close they

could see the tiny particles of soft black dust that patterned their wings. Harper couldn't remember ever seeing anything like them.

By the time they reached the cabin the butterflies were everywhere, swarming about them. Harper could feel the fanning of their tiny wings. One landed on his hand. Another on his shoulder. And another, and another. He looked at Moon. There were dozens of butterflies on Moon; on his head, on his arms and hands. One on his ear. One, beating its wings slowly, on his eye patch. A butterfly landed, momentarily, on Harper's nose, so that for a second he saw things crosseyed and flickering, as if he were watching an old-time movie. It fluttered away then, and his nose didn't even tickle.

Now all the butterflies were leaving. The one on Moon's ear, first. Then the one on his eye patch. The one on Harper's hand. The one nesting in Moon's hair. One after another, like tiny aircraft, they lifted off; circling around them, then drifting up, higher and higher, past the cabin eaves, past the mossy roof, higher than the chimney, up past the dark firs; the last afternoon sunlight turning them into gold and silver, so that they shone like new light in the sky.

Then they were gone.

Harper and Moon stood for a long time; dazzled, unable to move.

Finally Moon smiled. Not a grin. A smile. A true, goofy, happy smile.

"Olinger," he said softly, "saying good-bye."

Harper nodded. "Yes."

A thin white crescent of new moon showed overhead in the early evening sky. A squirrel scooted up a nearby fir and began its scolding. The smell of wood smoke hung in the air; the stove needed tending. It'd be cool, soon as night came on.

"Tell you what," Harper said. "How about heading down Bear Creek tomorrow morning, early? Catch us a mess of trout."